THE ICE CHIPS
AND THE
INVISIBLE PUCK

THE ICE CHIPS AND THE INVISIBLE PUCK

Roy MacGregor and Kerry MacGregor
Illustrations by Kim Smith

HarperCollins*PublishersLtd*

The Ice Chips and the Invisible Puck
Text copyright © 2019 by Roy MacGregor and Kerry MacGregor.
Illustrations copyright © 2019 by Kim Smith.

Published by HarperCollins Publishers Ltd

First published in Canada by HarperCollins Publishers Ltd
in a hardcover edition: 2019
This trade paperback edition: 2020

HarperCollins books may be purchased for educational, business,
or sales promotional use through our Special Markets Department.

HarperCollins Publishers Ltd
Bay Adelaide Centre, East Tower
22 Adelaide Street West, 41st Floor
Toronto, Ontario, Canada
M5H 4E3

www.harpercollins.ca

Library and Archives Canada Cataloguing in Publication

Title: The Ice Chips and the invisible puck / Roy MacGregor and Kerry MacGregor;
illustrated by Kim Smith.
Names: MacGregor, Roy, 1948- author. | MacGregor, Kerry, author. |
Smith, Kim, 1986- illustrator.
Description: Series statement: The Ice Chips series ; 3 | Previously published: 2019.
Identifiers: Canadiana 20200265172 | ISBN 9781443452359 (softcover)
Classification: LCC PS8575.G84 I34 2020 | DDC jC813/.6—dc23

Printed and bound in the United States of America
LSC/H 9 8 7 6 5 4 3 2 1

For Dayna Brons

—Roy MacGregor and Kerry MacGregor

For my beloved hometown, Calgary

—Kim Smith

CHAPTER 1
Location Unknown

Swift squeezed her eyes shut and tried desperately *not* to look down.

One of her hands was clinging to the cold metal railing beside her; the other held on desperately to one of Lucas Finnigan's hockey socks.

That sock—and Swift's grip on it—was the only thing keeping Lucas, now upside down, from sliding into the murky void that had suddenly appeared before them.

The young hockey players had leaped through time once again. And they couldn't believe *this* was where they'd landed: on a steep staircase, so high up in the air that they could be floating on a cloud!

"I'm NOT losing you *again*," Swift yelled, shivering in the darkness. She had no idea how this leap had gone so wrong, so fast, but she *was* sure of two things:

that her grip had better not slip, and that *she* was the one who'd brought them here.

"Top Shelf, you owe me," she'd said last night in the Ice Chips' dressing room, when she'd finally convinced Lucas (poor Lucas!) to take this leap. She'd leaned on him—pushed him—even when he swore he would never travel through time again.

But hadn't he expected her to do that? Everyone on the Ice Chips knew that when Nica "Swift" Bertrand wanted something, she went after it hard. That's how she'd made goalie for their hockey team year after year, even when some parents had insisted she should be playing sledge hockey instead. And that's how she'd figured out how to make saves with an adapted butterfly—so well that half the other teams didn't even know she had a prosthetic leg.

Swift was the one who'd wanted this leap; she'd been desperate for it. And now here they were . . . lost somewhere in time, and in trouble again.

"Whatever you do, don't wiggle! I'm going to try to pull you up!" Swift called down the steps, ignoring how quickly the icy wind carried her words away.

She was pulling on Lucas's sock as carefully as she could, but her heart was beating wildly. The moment they'd landed, she'd guessed they were high up—*really* high up. She'd felt it, even while her eyes were adjusting to the darkness. Her fear of heights was *that* strong.

It had all happened so fast. They'd crossed the centre line of their rink back in Riverton, after the ice had been resurfaced by Scratch and his magical flood, and then—*poof!*—they'd appeared here, stranded on this strange staircase . . . on a cold, wintry night.

"Ugh, we've leaped into the *dark* again?" Lucas had complained, turning to Swift just as his skate blade caught on one of the roughly carpeted steps and sent him flying.

Swift had called out as she'd reached for his gloved hand, but Lucas had missed his footing on the next step and continued to tumble. She was lucky her quick reflexes had helped her snag his sock before she'd lost him completely.

"Hey, help me! Give me your hand—*come on!*" Swift called back up the stairs to the other teammate who'd come with them.

If I keep my breathing even, she told herself, trying to ignore the sick feeling in her stomach, *we might get out of this alive.*

But Lucas's sock had begun to slip, and all Swift could hear from farther up the steps . . . was giggling!

"Stop it! Help me!" she called angrily toward Sadie—now known to the team as "Blades"—but her sister was laughing so hard she was doubled over.

"Does Lucas fall *every* time you leap?" Blades asked, letting the air out of her mouth like an over-inflated balloon.

Lucas, even upside down, turned beet red. He was trying not to move, but with his lungs breathing in the cold air, he, too, was soon shivering. Carefully, he shook off one of his hockey gloves, letting it fall beside him, and planted his hand down near his shoulder to keep from slipping.

He was surprised when, instead of touching another step, he found he'd put his hand down on something cold and wet. *Snow?*

"Ugh, Sadie! Give me your hand—NOW!" Swift yelled up the stairs again, at the exact moment when eight gigantic floodlights flashed on with a *shhh-thunk*, and a glistening white trail—the snow Lucas had half-landed on—was suddenly lit up beneath them.

Squinting in the bright lights, Swift could see that the snowy trail had two lines down the middle, like

two indented stripes, and at the end of it—way, way down below, where Lucas's glove had ended up—it scooped out, almost like the arc of a crescent moon. Even from up high, the trail looked like it was ready to launch anyone who dared go down it into outer space—probably into oblivion!

We're at the top of an Olympic ski jump?! Swift swallowed hard. The butterflies in her stomach were going nuts.

"No *waaaay*!" Lucas shouted as he looked down at the trail, almost forgetting that he was dangling there above it. When he turned back to Swift for her reaction, he finally saw a railing he could grab and went for it. Swift, who was in shock, could at last let go of his sock.

"Hey, Falls-a-lot. You gonna be okay there?" Blades asked Lucas, laughing at his expression of relief. "Maybe *you're* the one who should have stayed back at the ri—"

"*Shhhhh!*" Swift hissed, cutting her off. She was crouching on the stairs, as though it were possible to hide under those bright lights.

"*Shhhhh* what?" asked Blades, her voice still as loud as ever.

"I said *shhhhhhh*!" Swift hissed again. As quietly as she could, she moved down another step to Lucas, who was sitting beside the railing, unlacing his skates. "There's a *guy*," she whispered without turning her head.

"What guy?" Lucas asked, confused. He was still breathing heavily, trying to pretend he hadn't been scared.

"The guy. *That guy*," she whispered, motioning toward the steps on the other side of the trail.

There was now a man there, a little farther down and on a different set of steps, doing squats and throwing his arms out behind his back over and over again. He was in a blue ski suit and wore a helmet with pink goggles perched on top.

"Ready to give it a go!" the man called, in a British accent, to someone near the top of the jump.

Have they seen us?

Swift didn't think so, but it was hard to tell. She had no idea what might happen if they got caught.

Luckily, this man seemed to be concentrating hard. He was nervous—and excited.

"Now that's my kind of daredevil," Blades said with a mischievous smile, still not keeping her voice down. "I'd definitely take that jump."

"Blades—quiet!" Lucas warned as the skier scooted his butt along a wooden bench suspended between the two sets of steps and slipped his skis into the grooves in the snow.

"Oh no! He's not really going to—" Swift started, her stomach churning, but the skier was already checking the strap on his helmet and pulling his goggles down over his thick glasses. As he stood up on his skis, she again squeezed her eyes shut. There was no way she could watch this.

The skier bent forward as he let go and went sailing down the brightly lit trail with a loud scraping sound. *Swish!* He was gathering speed, fast. Then as he reached the end, the jump thrust him upward and launched him into the sky!

"He's flying!" Blades cheered, her voice bubbly, as she punched Swift in the arm. "I guess you wouldn't like the view from up there either!"

Swift was still angry with her sister about what had happened back in Riverton—about the argument they'd had before making this leap—but she knew she didn't have time to think about that now.

"You can breathe, Swift," Lucas told his teammate as the skier, wobbling a little, landed some distance away.

He was on his skis, but he was leaning too far to the right—and soon he was twisting . . . falling. As he hit the snow, sliding on his side, one ski was ripped from his foot. Enveloped in a wave of spraying snow, the jumper kept sliding until he skidded to a stop at the bottom of the hill, where the floodlights were still shining. Two onlookers immediately ran to check on him.

"He's okay!" said Blades, her eyes wild with excitement. *He was incredible!* The skier was soon jumping up all on his own, waving to tell everyone that he was he was fine. *What courage!*

Just the thought of what he'd done made Swift dizzy. But slowly, she opened her eyes and watched as the jumper, now standing, placed his hands on his knees. She imagined how heavily he had to be breathing— how scared she would have been.

"He's lucky he didn't break his leg on your glove on the way down," Blades said with a giggle as she opened her backpack and pulled out her boots, just as the others were doing. She pointed at the spot where Lucas's glove had come to rest. "I guess *that's* lost now."

Swift couldn't look. She kept her eyes on her skates as she zipped them into her backpack with the rest of her supplies.

"Ugh, that's my cousin Speedy's glove. My parents are going to kill—" Lucas started.

Just then, the bright floodlights flickered off, leaving them in the dark . . .

And then quickly banged on again.

"HEY! WHO'S UP THERE?!"

CHAPTER 2
Location Unknown

"RUN!"

All three Ice Chips yelled it at once.

Throwing their packs back over their shoulders, they moved as carefully and as quickly as they could down half a dozen of those very steep steps. Once they reached the bench the skier had used, they pulled themselves across it and onto the other staircase.

"There's an elevator!" Swift called out, pointing to the area above them—their only way out, unless they wanted to launch themselves off the end of the ski jump.

"Go for it!" Lucas shouted, grabbing Blades's arm and pulling her with him.

They still didn't know where that voice had come from—where the light control box was—but they didn't want to wait to find out.

"The button!" Lucas cried out as they neared the elevator. "PUSH IT!"

But Swift was already on it. The elevator arrived— empty, thank goodness—and they all piled in.

A moment later, they were gone.

* * *

"Why on earth did we land *there*?" Swift asked, confused, once they'd cleared the ski jump area and found their way to the gates of the Olympic Park. "That's not fair. *I'm* the one who chose this leap, and that's the *last* place I'd want to end up."

Swift could swear that up on those steps, she'd felt the jump drawing her toward it. It was the same feeling she'd had when the Riverton Ice Chips had visited Toronto's CN Tower—as if the void was trying to pull her over and swallow her up. Her sister had made her angry before the leap—angrier than she'd ever been—but now Swift was actually shaking. She'd never been so scared.

"Wait! Isn't that skier supposed to be your hero? The famous person you came here to meet?" Blades asked. She was out of breath, and she was still having trouble understanding how all this was supposed to work.

"I don't know if it can be just *any* athlete," said Swift, annoyed that she had to explain this to Blades, that she had to share the magic of this leap — *her* leap — with her little sister.

"That skier doesn't play hockey," said Lucas, trying to explain why Swift was so upset without making Blades feel bad. "We're still learning, but so far we've only met hockey players."

"It's GOTTA be a hockey player!" said Swift. "I mean, it's all about the rink, right?"

"Maybe — probably," Lucas answered. But he wasn't sure.

"Okay, then," said Blades, grabbing both of their arms and pulling them out of the park. "Let's go find a rink!"

* * *

"It's closed!" said Lucas. He pulled hard on the door of the large arena they'd found, not far from the Olympic Park. There was a metallic click, but it still wouldn't budge.

"What do we do now?" asked Blades, disappointed. "You got a skeleton key, or what?"

"I guess we wait," Swift said with a shrug. She took

the elastic out of her hair and retied her ponytail. "It's still nighttime. Maybe there's an early practice—or a late one? What is it . . . midnight?"

So far, Swift and Lucas had met Gordie Howe out on a frozen slough in Saskatchewan during the Depression, and Sidney Crosby in Halifax Harbour during a hurricane. But they hadn't gone *looking* for those hockey players—they'd just sort of . . . run into them.

"It's dangerous to be out in the cold overnight," Lucas warned. "We'll need to stay warm. If we can't get inside, we should walk around." He'd already pulled on a coat from his bag and was reaching into its pocket to grab his lucky quarter.

Swift's eyes immediately brightened. "What does your quarter say? What year?" she asked impatiently. *I need information! How else am I going to figure out who I'm supposed to meet?*

"You mean that nasty old quarter he rubs before every game? Yuck!" said Blades, her lips twisting into a frown. She still found most of Lucas's superstitions ridiculous—or gross. *Who wants to kiss a dusty old trophy case?*

"Yeah, *that* quarter," said Lucas, turning it over

in his hand. "We don't know how, but when we leap, it changes. Look . . . it's not from the 2010 Olympics anymore."

He was holding his arm outstretched so Blades could see what had happened to his lucky coin.

"Calgary, 1988," she read, as if it were no big deal— but of course it was. "And hey, there's a figure skater."

Lucas snapped his coin back to look at it again. *A figure skater? Does the coin look different to everyone?* What *he'd* seen were the Olympic rings and a goalie reaching out a gloved hand to make a save.

"Not on your stupid coin," said Blades, hitting Lucas's arm with the back of her hand and pointing to the parking lot. "This rink's for the figure skaters. And—oh, wow!—that's Elizabeth Manley!"

Swift put her hands on her hips as they watched the petite figure skater from Ottawa pull her skate bag out of the trunk of a car in the nearly empty parking lot, swing it over her shoulder, and start walking toward the rink with her coach.

"I just want to try that jump once more," the skater was telling her sleepy-eyed coach, who yawned as she pulled out a rink key. "Then we can go back to the hotel to sleep—promise."

"Do you remember these Olympics, Swift? I was just watching this at home!" Blades whisper-yelled. She was excited. "Liz Manley was an underdog, and no one expected her to do very well. But then she came out of nowhere and won the silver medal!"

Swift's heart sank as she watched a huge smile spread across her sister's face.

"I guess we're here to meet *my* hero!"

* * *

"It's not fair! It's not fair!" Swift repeated as Lucas and Blades followed her along one of the snowy streets that led away from the arena. She was angry and didn't care that she had no idea where she was going—or that it was still dark out.

"Turn around!" Blades complained. "We can get into the rink now!"

But Swift was making it obvious that she had no intention of meeting some superhero skater named Elizabeth Manley.

No one ever said we could control these leaps—or who we meet, Lucas thought. He felt sympathetic, but he also wished Swift weren't so upset. It wasn't like he'd *tried* to meet Sidney Crosby on their last leap—he'd just been lucky.

"Swift!" Blades yelled, grabbing on to her sister's arm. "Stop! Just wait a—"

"Whoa! If these are the Calgary Winter Games," Lucas blurted, suddenly remembering that he knew something about these competitions, too, "that British skier we saw must have been Eddie the Eagle. He's a *legend*. His country didn't have any other ski jumpers, and that's why he picked that sport! He made the team because he was the only one who signed up!"

"Good for him," snapped Swift, not sounding like herself.

"I mean, he was kind of a regular guy who just wanted to be in the Olympics. So he worked really hard and he did it!" Lucas continued, hoping this news might cheer her up. "My mom talks about him and how much he worked for this whenever I feel like quitting something."

"Of course she does," said Swift. Lucas had never seen her be so negative. "He's probably *her* hero, right? Maybe your mom should have come with us. I'm sure everyone's got a hero here but me!"

"What is *that*?" asked Blades, letting go of her sister's arm.

"Worst day of my life," answered Swift. She was finally ready to continue the fight they'd started back home—a fight the two sisters had never had before, but one that had been brewing since the beginning of the hockey season. "Why do you have to be here anyway, Sadie? This is *my* leap!"

"No—ugh, Nica!" said Blades. "I'm not talking about *you*. I'm talking about *that*!"

There was a sound. A strange sound. A scraping sound, but not always scraping. A scrape, then silence, then a scrape, then another, another, another.

Neither Swift nor Lucas could figure out where it was coming from.

"There aren't . . . aliens in the bushes here, are there?" Blades asked, completely serious. "It's coming from that backyard—between those two houses."

"*Shhhh*," said Swift, before quietly creeping between the houses so she could peer through a hedge.

The twin backyards were pitch black, or so it seemed, and around the blackness, someone had strung up some kind of thick, dark netting. Looking up, Swift could see only the odd star in the sky, until

the clouds slowly allowed the moon to break through and a soft white light fell over the large surface that covered the two backyards.

A rink!

And there was someone on it!

The scraping sound was skates, and it got louder when the person on the ice turned and dug in, skating harder.

Scrape . . .

Scrape . . .

Scrape, scrape . . .

SCRAPE . . .

"Why's that kid out there in the middle of the night?" Blades asked, this time quietly, as she and Lucas snuck up beside Swift. They'd pushed their way through the hedge and were now all breathing foggy air through the netting at the edge of the rink. "There's not enough light out yet—how can that kid even see the puck?"

"*She can't*," said Swift, her heart suddenly beating faster.

CHAPTER 3
Riverton, A Few Days Earlier

It was December in Riverton. The days had grown shorter, but even with the deep snow and the icicles on the roof edges, Lucas, Swift, and Ekamjeet Singh—"Edge"—had been happy to walk in the dark to their after-school practice. This was, after all, turning out to be a great year. The Ice Chips, now completely settled back into their old Riverton Community Arena, had just moved into first place in the league!

"Yeah! Do it again!" Tianna "Bond" Foster shouted as Blades took another tour around the rink, pulled her stick in tight, and did a loose axel jump—in hockey skates!—before scooping up a puck.

Both Bond and Lars Larsson cheered, but Swift had to stop herself from rolling her eyes. This was the Ice Chips' last practice before their next game against

the Riverton Stars, and she was getting tired of watching her sister show off.

That isn't even hockey!

Coach Small had asked the Ice Chips to practise their shots for a few minutes while he talked to Quiet Dave the Iceman, the rink's maintenance guy, and of course he hadn't told them *how* to take those shots. Lucas, the Chips' biggest hockey nut, was taking the assignment seriously, but Bond and Blades were just fooling around.

"How does your sister not trip on her stick?" Maurice Boudreau, the big defenceman known as "Slapper," asked Swift as he grabbed a puck from behind the net. The Chips' goalie just shrugged and banged her stick on the ice, letting her teammates know she was ready for more shots.

This next game against the Stars, their arch rivals and the only other competitive novice team in town, was a big one. The two teams had already met four times in the season, and each had won two games. The Chips were still four points ahead of the Stars—and Swift, Edge, and Lucas knew they'd have to work hard to keep it that way.

"C'mon, let's go! Keep sending 'em over!" Swift called out.

Lucas fired a wrist shot that slipped in over her shoulder—her weak spot. Then Edge scooped up a puck and fired it, but she blocked it easily.

"Ugh! Why are my shots so *hoser-ific* this week?" Edge shouted before hooking the bounce and looping around again.

Another shot. Another miss.

"You'll get it," said Lucas, as he went for a slap-shot. He'd had the same problem at the beginning of the season; he knew how Edge was feeling.

Swift and Lucas had been out practising behind Riverton P.—what they called Riverton Public School—all week. Coach Small—called "Mr. Small" when he was their teacher in class—had got together with some of the parents and created a little outdoor rink there so the kids could skate whenever they wanted. Thanks to that extra ice time, Swift was feeling better than ever about her glove hand, and Lucas almost had his beauty shot—the one where he knocked the puck out of the air like Sidney Crosby and slammed it into the back of the net—down completely. In practice, at least.

But Edge hadn't come out at all.

Now, seeing their friend at this Chips' practice, Swift thought she knew why: Edge had lost his touch.

He was still leading the league in scoring, but that could easily change with the next game. Jared Blitz, the Stars' nasty centre, was behind Edge by only a single point, followed closely by his sister, Beatrice. If Edge couldn't find the net, one of the Blitz twins might take the lead.

He's in a slump, she thought, not daring to say it out loud.

Swift needed her team to win—this year, more than ever. Especially now that Beatrice Blitz, the Stars' cheating, pushing, bullying forward, had decided to make the Chips' goalie her new target.

At the beginning of the season, Beatrice had set her sights on Lucas, even sabotaging his skates, but now she was going after Swift—every single chance she got. Swift hated Beatrice and hated playing against her, but she'd do it if that was the only way her team could make the playoffs—and maybe even win the trophy this year.

Of course, no one could love that trophy as much as Lucas. He was the one who had to kiss the Chips' display case each time he walked into the arena, as part of his superstitious ritual. There wasn't even a trophy in the case—just an old faded photograph of some long-ago Ice Chips celebrating their one and only trophy win. Lucas liked to imagine he was one of the two ten-year-old boys holding the trophy high above their heads in the photo; Swift just wanted to *play the game* that won it.

"Okay, that's enough!" Coach Small called to his players as he stepped up to the boards, followed by Quiet Dave and Abigail Ward, who was the mayor of Riverton, but also Dave's daughter.

Blades was sailing by with her leg out behind her in an arabesque, while Lars, giggling, swooped in and surprised Swift by going five-hole. Swift was so annoyed that she tossed her stick onto the ice.

"Everyone gets a last shot," said Coach Small. "Then we'll change it up." He banged twice on the boards and gave the Chips' goalie a stern look.

Sheepishly, Swift picked up her stick and moved back into her crease.

"Bond, Blades . . . and Swift," the coach added, "when everyone's done, you three then come over to the boards for a chat."

Swift, now sure she was in trouble, stayed in net while Dylan Chung—called "Mouth Guard" by his teammates because he didn't have a filter between his brain and his tongue—and Sebastián Strong—the human calculator known as "Crunch"—took their shots.

Lucas went for another slapshot—this time, even Mayor Ward applauded—and then last was Edge, who was still struggling. He went for a wrister, but it bounced off, just like the one before it.

No one said anything as Bond, Blades, and Swift finally skated over to the boards with their heads down.

"Swift was in net the whole time. She was *working*," Lucas protested from where he was gathering pucks. The Chips' centre knew that when someone got in trouble, Coach Small sometimes had that player sit out for an entire game. He also knew that the Ice Chips needed their best goalie.

The coach looked up at Lucas for a second, but then turned back to the three players who now stood in front of him.

"It seems that Beatrice Blitz and her father—well, Coach Blitz—have come to the mayor with a proposal," he started slowly. Swift scanned his face, but he wasn't giving any clue as to what that proposal could be. "And . . . uh, the mayor wants to know how you girls feel about it."

How we feel *about it?* Swift was confused. *Does this mean we're not in trouble?*

"So far, it's just an idea," began Mayor Ward,

pushing her fluffy auburn bangs to the side and adjusting the pair of glasses she had in her pocket. "Next month, Hopedale will be holding its annual novice girls' tournament."

Girls' tournament?! Bond and Blades turned to Swift immediately. There was no girls' team in Riverton—even the Chips' rookies knew that.

"And . . . well," the mayor continued, "we were hoping you girls might win us the cup!"

* * *

The next night, for a game at the gaudy new Blitz Sports Complex, Coach Small was wearing earplugs.

The arena was almost as loud as it had been on opening night. Hard rock music screamed from the loudspeakers and lights flashed from the Jumbotron as the Stars made their way onto the ice. No surprise that Coach Blitz—the richest and most full-of-himself man in Riverton—was grinning at his players from the bench.

He loves it when his *Stars play in* his *arena*, Lucas thought as he watched the coach tip his baseball cap to his twins, Jared and Beatrice, who were taking their positions on the Stars' side.

Coach Small waited until the sound died down before he sent his Ice Chips out. He told them, as he always did, just to try their best and remember to "keep it simple."

"Don't try anything too complicated out there," he reminded them with a smile as they came through the chute. "Keep your eyes on the puck and remember to KISS—keep it simple, stupid."

"We know, *KISS!!*" the Chips shouted back at him, giggling and rolling their eyes.

"*KIIIIIIIIIIIIIISSSSSSS!*"

Mouth Guard, as usual, made a kissy fish face, nearly tripping Lucas as they moved through the door in the boards.

The Chips stepped onto the ice to a smattering of cheers from their families and fans, and some hearty boos from the Stars' fans. They were now used to this rowdy reception at their opponents' rink. In a way, they even liked it. It fired them up. It felt like the NHL. And what could be sweeter than a win on the Stars' home ice?

Of course, today that might be a long shot.

Edge, their best scorer, was still unsure of himself—both Swift and Lucas could tell. At practice, he'd been panicking with the puck, hurrying his shots and passes, not thinking. He couldn't seem to relax. If he looked up, he lost the puck. If he didn't look up, he made bad blind passes and giveaways. The last thing he was doing was keeping it simple.

"Hey, if this doesn't work out, I'll just become an announcer—do the play-by-play for the games," Edge had joked to Lucas and Crunch in the car on the way to the rink. "Check it out: *He shoots and he never scores!!*"

Coach Small, who was driving, had told Edge that he had to be patient, that slumps are something everyone goes through. He'd even told him a story about one of the old Ottawa Senators, Bruce Gardiner, who once managed to break out of a long scoring slump by taking his stick into the washroom and trying to flush it down the toilet.

"Next game," Coach Small said with a chuckle, "half the team was in there flushing their sticks."

Lucas laughed and decided he'd probably try it, but he knew Edge wouldn't. Edge didn't believe in magic or superstitions.

Just to be safe, their coach was now starting Lucas on the line with Mouth Guard and Lars Larsson, and had moved Edge to the second line with Blades and Alex Stepanov—the little Russian-speaking kid called "Dynamo."

Swift was surprised to see Lucas and Lars on the same line again, but ever since they'd teamed up together at the grand opening of the Blitz arena, she knew Lucas felt that he and Lars had real chemistry on the ice. They were no longer enemies; they were teammates. And Coach Small — he felt that, too.

Coach Blitz was of course starting his children's line: Jared at centre ice, Beatrice on one wing, and a rough-and-tumble kid named Darryl on the other. They had proved to be the best line in the district this year — something Beatrice made sure to tell Swift *every* time she saw her.

Beatrice snarled as Swift moved into her crease. The Chips' goalie banged her stick against her pads as she always did to say she was ready — even though she knew she was going to have trouble keeping her head in the game.

Swift couldn't stop thinking about yesterday's conversation with the mayor.

Hopedale, a bigger town, had asked if Riverton would like to send a novice girls' team over to compete in their annual day-long tournament for girls. The problem was always the same: Riverton had no girls' team to send. But this year, Coach Blitz and Beatrice had come up with the idea of an "all-star team" made up of the best girls playing in Riverton, taken from both the competitive and the house league teams. There weren't all that many girls playing, but together there would be enough.

They'd form a one-time team, just for this competition.

Swift was thinking about this—the absolute *worst* idea she'd ever heard—when the puck dropped.

Soon, the Stars were ahead on a sweet goal by Jared Blitz. He'd done a toe drag around Bond and snapped a quick shot high over Swift's shoulder. Less than two minutes later, the Ice Chips tied it up when Lucas took a gamble on Lars reading his mind and cranked a lead pass off the boards. Lars, in full flight, caught up to the puck for a clear breakaway. He came in on the Stars' goaltender, went forehand to backhand, and roofed a goal in off the crossbar.

The two teams exchanged goals three times after that, heading into the final five minutes of stop time in a 4–4 tie.

But then Bond made a mistake on a clearing shot. She meant to send it high off the glass, but accidentally shot it too high, so the puck sailed up into the stands. *KISS*—she'd forgotten it. The referee's whistle blew and his right arm swept out from his side: delay of game, two-minute penalty.

That gave the Stars a power play at the worst possible moment. Coach Blitz and his assistant bumped fists and laughed—they couldn't believe their luck. The Chips would be playing short-handed during Bond's penalty, with almost no chance to win the game. The Stars would have five shooters to the Ice Chips' four, and with that advantage, they'd have several chances to win.

Coach Small sent out his four best checkers: Dynamo, Lucas, Edge, and Slapper. Swift set herself in goal, rapping her stick hard against her posts—her "friends"—and then coming far out into her crease in a crouch position, glove hand out and ready to snare any puck that dared threaten her net.

Beatrice Blitz won the faceoff over Edge and got the puck back to Jared so he could play the point on the power play with his hard shot.

But instead, Jared dumped the puck into the corner so Lucas would have to get it away from two big Stars players. As Lucas and those two big kids collided together against the boards, Jared slyly looped around, making his way toward the puck again. That's when Lucas felt the butt end of the mean centre's stick jab sharply into his gut, taking his breath away. Gasping, he kept working as Jared skated away again. Now, the two big players were definitely too much for him. The Stars came out of the corner cycling the puck—dropping it back when threatened and then back again—until they reached Beatrice Blitz, who then joined the cycle.

Lucas knew he should be there to check her, but he couldn't catch his breath. It felt like someone had lit a blowtorch in his lungs.

Carrying the puck, Beatrice drove hard to the net. She fired a shot, and Swift gloved the black disc . . . but then dropped it.

The Chips' goalie fell on her knees, pads covering the puck.

But Beatrice kept coming. She bowled Swift over, spinning her, legs splaying, off to the side.

Lucas saw the puck lying there like it was the only thing on the empty ice. He knew he was closest and should leap on it, but he couldn't move. He still couldn't catch his breath.

Jared Blitz, following his sister in, quickly tapped the puck into the open side of the net.

The Riverton Stars had won.

CHAPTER 4

Swift's face was red, and everyone in the dressing room could see that she was angry with herself. No one said a word. There was nothing to say. The Stars' win had closed the gap between the two teams, and they were now tied for the league lead. Beatrice Blitz, with two goals and three assists, had moved ahead of her brother in scoring, but she'd also moved ahead of Edge by a point. The league's meanest player now had the scoring lead.

Lucas was still trying to breathe normally—he felt like his rib cage had been crushed—when Coach Small came in to talk to them.

"Good effort, kids," said the coach. "Excellent effort. It was just a fluke thing that gave them that power play at a bad time. Hockey happens. There's nothing you can do about it."

Coach Small looked at Bond, who seemed upset, and winked.

"Oh, and Swift, Blades, Bond—let's have another quick word before you leave, okay?"

The three Ice Chips looked at each other. Bond and Blades gave each other high-fives—they loved this idea of a Riverton girls' team—but Swift couldn't wipe the scowl from her face.

❊　❊　❊

"NO WAY!" said Swift. "Absolutely *no way* in the world. Never. EVER!"

Lucas had never seen Swift so upset.

He and the rest of the boys on the Ice Chips team had waited for the three girls to finish their post-game meeting with Coach Small. Mouth Guard figured it was about Bond's shooting the puck over the glass and taking a penalty that had cost them the game. He shut his mouth when Lucas pointed out that the players asked to stay back were the same three who had been asked to play for the Hopedale Novice Girls' Cup.

When they came out, Blades and Bond both seemed excited. But not Swift.

"They're saying they *need* me on the team," Swift told the boys. "They said I *have to* play with Coach Blitz's horrible spoiled daughter—sorry, Lars—or else they won't have a goalie!"

Even though Lars was the Blitz twins' cousin, he knew that what Swift was saying about Beatrice wasn't wrong.

"And of course, whatever rich little Beatrice wants, she gets. Right?" Swift moaned, kicking her hockey bag so hard that her goalie stick slid off it and clattered to the ground.

"Come on, Swift," Bond said. "It'll be us, the girls from the Stars team, and a few house players. Kinda cool to be all girls—almost like being back in roller derby."

"Bond!" grunted Swift. "You saw what happened out there tonight. Beatrice tried to take me out."

"Actually," corrected Blades, "she *did* take you out. But so what? This is hockey. I can't wait to play in this tournament!"

"You don't even *know* hockey," Swift said with venom in her voice.

"Swift, can't you just—" Lucas started, but then he stopped. He loved hockey just like Swift, but he knew only the girls could decide what playing on this new team would mean to them.

"Look, you two can say yes," Swift said, not even looking Bond and Blades in the eyes, "but I'm saying no. Beatrice Blitz is the dirtiest player in the league, and I will never play on *any* hockey team with her. *Ever!*"

* * *

Swift had never felt such pressure.

She *knew* she was the only girl who played goal in Riverton. She also knew that Coach Small had tried to put it delicately when he'd warned her that Mayor Ward wanted an answer by the end of the week.

This was big. It was also why Swift had asked Lucas to meet her here, between school and their next practice, at his parents' WhatsIt Shop. She knew she couldn't handle this all on her own.

"Lucas wants to know if you want whipped cream on top," Mrs. Finnigan said as she leaned into the bay window behind Swift's chair and removed a potted plant that was no longer doing well—one of the final details in the WhatsIt Shop's new makeover.

In the last few months, the Finnigans' store had finally come to life. Thanks to Mrs. Finnigan's idea of putting a few chairs and tables in the front window, new customers were showing up to sip coffee and munch on homemade cookies. They soon found themselves wandering up and down the aisles, investigating the wonders that were tucked away in the bins and baskets the Finnigans had stacked on the shelves — "bits and bobs for the oddest jobs," according to their motto. Swift liked to think of the store as one giant junk drawer, but she also thought it was one of the coolest places in town.

"No whipped cream, thanks," she said, resting her chin in the palm of her hand. She was reading a sign taped to the window explaining that, starting tomorrow, the store would host a weekly "fix-it club," where volunteers could meet to drink coffee and fix other people's broken objects for free.

"So I can guess why you buzzed me," Lucas said solemnly, arriving with two hot chocolates on a tray and glancing down at his comm-band — the walkie-talkie-like bracelet the Ice Chips used to communicate with each other.

Lucas knew the mayor had been on Swift's case —

the local newspaper, too—and even her parents seemed to be pressuring her.

He sat down beside his friend, pushing a cup toward her, but she didn't appear to notice its existence. She was looking out the window. She was lost.

"I want to say no—I *really* want to say no," said Swift. "But it seems that everyone's already decided I'm playing in that tournament. It's not fair."

"Well, why don't you say yes? It sounds awesome," Lucas said. He took a sip of his hot chocolate but decided it was too hot. "Is it just because of Beatrice?"

"Mostly—definitely," Swift admitted with a shrug. "But it's . . . my sister, too."

"Blades is like your best friend," he said, unable to stop himself from trying his hot chocolate again. Still too hot.

"Yeah, she is—I mean, she *was*," groaned Swift. She didn't quite know how to say it. She was embarrassed to let the thought escape her lips. "But hockey used to be just my sport—*my thing*—and now it's hers, too. And that's *hard*. Is that awful of me?"

"A little awf—" Lucas started, but he could see his mom coming back with two new plants to place in the window.

"Oh, Swift! That Hopewell tournament will be great, won't it?" said Mrs. Finnigan, smiling and looking at the Chips' goalie. "I always wanted to be in it when I used to play. But in those days we definitely didn't have enough Riverton girls to make up a team!"

"She's not going," Lucas said impulsively, which got him a kick under the table.

"I'm thinking about it!" Swift lied with an awkward smile.

"You should do it. It's a great opportunity," Mrs. Finnigan said, almost singing as she made her way back to the cash to ring in another customer.

"Why did you—" Swift asked in a loud whisper. "Can everyone just—wait, what's *this*?"

Edge, Mouth Guard, and Crunch had suddenly appeared behind Lucas. The first two had snow on their shoulders, but Crunch had obviously been walking around in the store: both hands were filled with bits and bobs, and he had a tin cookie pan tucked under one arm.

"I buzzed them while I was getting the hot chocolates," Lucas said, worried Swift would be mad. "We don't mean to push you, but we all think you should play."

"You, too? Guys! My answer is no!" said Swift, slamming her hand down so hard that the chocolate from both drinks splashed onto the table. "I refuse to play with that girl. She hates me and I hate her. You saw what she tried to do to me. She ran me in last night's game. There's no worse thing you can do in hockey."

"I don't get it—*what's wrong* with the tournament?" asked Mouth Guard, who hadn't been paying attention.

"If you play, I'll call the game for you," Edge said with a smile. "Goooooaaaal! Goooooooaal! GOOOOAAAAL-LEE-OOOH-LEEE-OOO! *Right?* I mean—not on your net, though."

Swift just rolled her eyes. She'd had enough.

"Saying yes would mean sitting in the same dressing room as my enemy," Swift grumbled. "Don't you get that?"

"Lucas plays with Lars now," Edge said with a shrug of his shoulders.

"Sometimes Lars is kind of great," Lucas admitted with a smile.

"Well, Beatrice will never be great," said Swift, still arguing. "I hate her."

"You said that," muttered Mouth Guard as he grabbed a chair and pulled Swift's hot chocolate toward him. He'd decided she wasn't going to drink it; she was spending too much time yelling.

"I've got to get out of here! I'll see you at practice," Swift said, trying to get past Crunch so she could grab her coat. "Ugh! Why do you have all this stuff with you?"

"It's for tomorrow's fix-it club," Crunch answered proudly. He was almost vibrating he was so excited. "Lucas's mom and Quiet Dave are going to teach us how to fix things, build things—it's going to be the greatest."

"Wait! Quiet Dave will be at the store?" Swift said with her eyebrows twisted. Lucas had never seen her so interested. "And he'll be here *all evening*?"

Lucas took the final sip of his hot chocolate, not daring to speak. *She couldn't really be thinking . . .*

Swift was looking at Crunch, Mouth Guard, and Edge. "If you can keep Dave here tomorrow night, and make sure he doesn't come back to the rink," she said, lowering her voice and ignoring the fact that Lucas was shaking his head, "then I've got a plan."

CHAPTER 5

The first part of the plan belonged to the Ice Chips' goalie—just as it had the two other times they'd leaped. It made sense: Swift was the only one who could get her dad's rink keys.

Once school was done the next day, she took off running as fast as she could to beat her dad home. Getting out of Riverton, even if she had to do it with the help of a rink-flooding time machine, was the only answer that made sense now. And she couldn't afford to get caught.

When Swift arrived at the house, her sister was already in the living room, watching old figure skating videos.

"Can you imagine if I'd stayed in figure skating? I'd be skating on Blitz's plastic rink *every day*—awful," Blades called. "I'm *so* glad I switched to hockey."

"Yeah, me, too," Swift lied, trying to sound normal—trying not to draw attention to herself. She didn't want Blades to find out what she and Lucas were about to do.

"Are you sure you're *happy* I'm on the team?" Blades asked suspiciously. She looked quickly at Swift and then turned her head back toward the television. The skater had just pulled off a big jump and everyone was clapping.

Swift saw her moment and moved quickly, slipping into her dad's office without a sound. The girls' father usually worked until dinnertime—which was soon. Their mom was already home, but she was all the way upstairs, talking on the phone.

"You were scowling at me like a grump-a-lump last practice," Blades called from the couch. She was feeling braver now that Swift was in the other room. "Grump-a-lump" was the one word Edge had invented that had finally caught on.

"I wasn't. I just—" Swift yelled from the office. She knew she should leave it alone, but she couldn't. "Well, why do you have to do *everything* I do?"

"What, you mean playing stupid hockey?" Blades barked back, hurt.

46

"If you think it's so stupid, why are you playing at all? Hockey's *my* sport!" said Swift, her voice shaking a little.

She knew she shouldn't be arguing with her sister while looking for her dad's keys, but she couldn't help herself. She hadn't found them yet—her dad must have moved them—and that had put her on edge. All she'd found in his desk was a handful of paper clips.

"Look, you don't have to be so jealous that I—" Blades called from the living room, but she stopped when she heard their father's car pull into the driveway.

Panicked, Swift scanned the office as fast as she could, until—finally!—she spotted the keys in a small glass jar on the bookshelf.

She was carefully closing the door to the office behind her—she was almost there—when suddenly her heart jumped into her throat: her sister was standing in the hallway in front of her, her bare feet firmly planted on the cold tile floor.

With her arms crossed, Blades glanced down at the keys in Swift's hand and then over at the front door, where their father was turning his key.

Swift looked back at her, pleading.

"I won't tell," Blades said under her breath as the door swung open. "But you're taking me with you."

* * *

Blades wasn't on the ice when Lucas, Edge, and Swift had first travelled through time. She was *close to* the rink—outside, getting caught by Quiet Dave for sneaking into the arena with her friends—but she never saw any of the magic. She didn't *know* what had happened.

"Lucas. *Lucas!*" Swift whispered now, as she and her sister moved toward the bushes at the arena's entrance.

When Lucas popped his head up, he was surprised to see that Blades had tagged along. Swift dismissed his questions with an apologetic shrug and was soon unlocking the arena door.

"We're in!"

"All clear this time?" Blades asked Lucas with a smirk, remembering the fight they'd had with Quiet Dave the last time. "So what's the plan—just skating?"

"I'll . . . uh, tell you inside," Lucas said, looking at Blades suspiciously.

"My pushy sister's not going to leave early this time," said Swift as the heavy arena door closed behind them. "We might as well tell her everything."

＊　＊　＊

Lucas is the one who told Blades about their first leap into the past—about Scratch, the little ice resurfacer they'd found, and how shocked they were when they'd realized his floods were magical. He described how they'd unknowingly skated across the centre line . . . and then—*poof*!

Once they'd changed into their hockey gear, Swift explained the rest.

"It's like a portal opens up or something," she said, unable to hide her excitement.

"Like a door," added Lucas. "That's how we ended up in the Prairies in a snowstorm, and how, the next time, we appeared in the middle of a hurricane in Halifax Harbour."

"Sounds awful," said Blades, but there was a smile on her face. She loved anything that sounded dangerous. "Where are we going on *this* leap?"

"Honestly?" asked Lucas.

Swift answered: "We have absolutely no idea."

* * *

Lucas was ready first. He stood by the open door, watching the ceiling lights ripple yellow as the fresh flood hardened. He loved this ice. Edge and Crunch kept saying that science had made this happen, but Lucas had his own idea: it had to be magic.

Swift led the way as the three players—backpacks on, hockey sticks in hand—stepped out onto the shining surface. They could all feel the hard, fresh ice through their blades. It was perfect.

Lucas took a stride and turned sharply at the end of it, his skates cutting through the fresh flood with a sound like steak being seared on his grandfather's grill.

Swift cut hard with her skates, testing the ice, too.

Blades was last, her eyes as wide as hockey pucks.

"EVERYONE READY?" Lucas asked loudly— the rink was empty, after all.

"Ready!" the two girls called back.

"We start out together," Swift said, turning toward

her sister. "And we stick together. From the blue line on, there's no turning back—understood?"

"Understood," said Blades, grinning.

As the three Chips zipped across the centre line holding hands, there was a flash.

And a sound. A whirring—no, blowing. Like a cold wind whistling by their ears.

The light grew brighter . . . and brighter . . .

And then, all of a sudden . . .

Everything went black.

CHAPTER 6
Calgary, Alberta–Back to the Leap!

None of the Ice Chips had ever seen anything like it.

"How can she do that in the *dark*?" Lucas asked in awe.

The clouds had shifted a little more, and Swift, Lucas, and Blades could now perfectly see the young hockey player's outline on the backyard rink in front of them. The girl was skating and had a stick that she was moving back and forth, up and down the ice.

They could hear the scraping of her skates, but they couldn't hear a thing from her stickhandling.

Does she even have *a puck? Or is she just pretending she's got one?* Lucas couldn't tell. All he knew was that he was witnessing something unbelievable.

Swift was watching, too, but she was also staring at the large, perfectly groomed surface the skater with the invisible puck was gliding across. It was the greatest backyard rink any of the Ice Chips had ever seen. These neighbours with adjoining backyards, whoever they were, had done a spectacular job. Their rink was about half the size of a regulation one. It had small boards all around it, and if she squinted, Swift thought she could see a red line and two blue ones painted on it. In the daylight, this rink must almost look official.

The girl on the ice leaned out like she was reaching for a puck that was getting away, but turned it into a slapshot—one that smacked against the boards right where the three Ice Chips were standing.

Craaaaaa-ACK!

They all jumped back. Her shot, even in the dark, was incredible.

"Hey, you guys wanna play?" the girl called over in their direction. They could hear in her voice that she was smiling.

"Uh, yeah," said Lucas, opening his coat to show that he was still wearing his jersey—even though he knew she could barely see it.

"Definitely," said Swift, raising her goalie stick in the air.

With a nod from the player on the ice, the Chips

bent down, pulled their skates out of their bags, and eagerly laced them up.

Why not? thought Swift. *We don't have anything else to do while we're waiting for* my *Olympic hero to show up!*

❊   ❊   ❊

"I can't see it. I mean . . . I really *can't* see it," said Lucas, looking down at the ice in front of his skates, where the puck was supposed to be. "Can't we turn on the rink lights?"

"We have the stars," said the girl. "That's all we'll need."

"The stars aren't bright enough," said Blades, who was tracing teardrop shapes on the ice with her skates. She couldn't see the puck either.

"No, that's not what I mean," the girl replied. Again, they could tell she was grinning.

Soon she'd hooked her arms in theirs and was slowly skating them over toward Swift, who was moving into one of the rink's nets. The girl, who was around ten, had already told them not to shout—warned them that they shouldn't wake up the rink's owners.

Are any of us actually supposed to be here? Swift had wondered.

"Look up for a second!" the girl said, eagerly tapping the goalie's arm. Swift pulled her mask up so it was sitting on top of her head, then tilted her face toward the sky.

"Hey, there's Orion," Blades said, pointing to a grouping of pinpoints of light in the darkness above.

"And the Big D—*uh*, Dipper," Lucas added, trying to keep his voice down. This was the only star formation he knew, mostly because his brother, Connor, called it the Big Diaper. Who could forget that?

"Over there is the planet Venus," the girl said excitedly. "You can tell because it's low in the sky, it's very bright, and the light doesn't change—planets don't twinkle like stars.

"Anyone want to wish on a star?" giggled Blades. "There are a million of them!"

Thinking about the tunnel through time they'd used to get here, Lucas wanted to ask, "Can you see a wormhole?"—that's what Edge had called it—but he knew he shouldn't.

"Oh, yeah—and I'm Chicken," the girl said, touching gloves with the three kids from Riverton.

Chicken? Swift repeated in her head, almost giggling. She'd never heard such a funny nickname.

* * *

A very light snow began to fall as Chicken plopped four pucks down on the black ice surface in front of the Chips. The flat, round discs seemed to vanish, their colour blending in so perfectly with the dark, dark ice. Even when Lucas looked straight down, the pucks seemed invisible.

Chicken took off immediately with one of them, effortlessly skating and stickhandling down the ice. Again, the only sound the Chips could hear was the scraping of her blades on the cold, dark surface below her.

Excited, Swift picked up a stick that was resting on top of the net so she could try it, too. She *had* to— what Chicken was doing was such a cool trick!

The Chips' goalie felt the puck on her blade. It felt firm and real. She stickhandled back and forth, the puck moving smoothly from the front of the blade to the back, and from the back to the front. She began skating, the cold night air stinging her cheeks. She kept her face up, as Chicken had instructed, and as both Lucas and Blades were now doing in their own corners of the rink. Swift even looked up at the stars from time to time—and was amazed to see that the puck stayed with her!

I can feel *it*, she thought—wondering for a moment if she should have been a forward instead. *What a great skill for an out player to have, but how will this help me in net?*

She did know one player it *would* help, but he was all the way back in Riverton.

Edge should be here, Lucas was thinking, too, as he moved up and down the ice, sliding his own puck back and forth. *I don't even have to look at what I'm doing! I'm looking straight up into the dark, but I can still see the stick and the puck in my mind!*

Suddenly, the two Chips both knew what their team's star forward needed to do to get out of his slump: stop skating with his head down so much. Coach Small had told them to keep it simple and to keep their eyes on the black disc, but Edge, under pressure to stay on top, had taken that too seriously. If he looked up more, he'd see what was coming and would stop panicking with the puck! That was it!

"Okay!" Chicken shouted from across the ice, forgetting her own rule to be quiet. "Now give *me* your pucks!"

Lucas, Swift, and Blades all passed their pucks across to her, and she flipped each one up by the blade of her stick and caught it before it fell back on the ice. She then placed their three pucks on top of the net.

"Let's try reading each other!" Chicken called out.

She took off with her remaining puck, stickhandling softly back toward them. The Chips, all of them trying to use their other senses like their new friend, could hear the sizzle of her skates on the hard black ice and a bare whisper of sound as she moved the puck from side to side.

Chicken had her head up and saw everyone—their outlines, at least. Swift had moved back into net with her goalie stick, and Lucas was now racing across the ice to pick up Chicken's perfect backhand pass. He felt the puck tap his stick as he snared it, and then he began skating and stickhandling—just like she had!

He *sensed* rather than *saw* Blades moving behind him, and he dropped a pass between his own skates that Blades picked up easily.

Chicken rapped her stick on the ice in admiration.

Blades got the puck back to Lucas and he turned sharply, sending a saucer pass that floated through the air like a Frisbee and then slapped onto the ice just ahead of Swift's skates. He wasn't sure if he was actually supposed to shoot it on Swift's net in the dark—or if that would be too dangerous for her. That was something he'd have to ask their expert.

Swift lurched forward, her stick held out across her body, but she wasn't even sure where the puck had landed. *Does this trick of not seeing the puck even work for goalies?* she wondered.

"Perfect!" Chicken shouted. "You've got it, Lucas and Blades! You've got it!"

"Wait, what about m—" Swift started. But suddenly, a light flicked on in what had to be one of the neighbours' kitchens.

Soon, a back door was sliding open.

"What the—?!" a man's sleepy voice called out.

Swift, Lucas, and Blades looked back in fear as the man stumbled out the door, rubbing his hands together to keep warm. He flicked on one of the small floodlights that had been fastened around the backyard rink, momentarily blinding the Chips and their new friend.

"CHICKEN!" the man called out, obviously surprised. He was standing on his back steps in his pyjamas and slippers, and he had his arms crossed while he shivered. "It's 3 a.m.! You're going to miss the tournament tomorrow!"

"Your dad calls you Chicken, too?" asked Blades, leaning on her stick.

"He's not my dad," said Chicken, but she didn't have time to explain any further.

"And you other kids—go back to your billet families! It's the final game tomorrow!" the man ordered, his breath escaping his body like a fog. Then he slipped back into the house and closed the door, leaving it unlocked for the young hockey player who was supposed to be inside, tucked tightly into her sleeping bag on their living room floor. Their guest.

Blades and Lucas looked at each other. *Go back where?*

"He won't get you in trouble," said Chicken, looking embarrassed. "My billet house is great—really, the Desmonds are amazing. Well . . . but you guys snuck out, too, right?"

"Yeah, of course," said Swift. It wasn't a complete lie. Chicken had already told her about the tournament while the other two were practising with their invisible pucks. Swift had never said they were part of it, but she hadn't said they *weren't* either.

"I guess we all need sleep," said Chicken, rolling her eyes. "It is, you know, the middle of the night!"

"Yeah, we should be going," said Blades, who was now wondering if they might be able to find Elizabeth Manley's hotel. Maybe they'd even be able to watch her compete.

"You'll be at the tournament tomorrow morning? The mini-Olympics?" Chicken asked eagerly as they all started unlacing their skates.

"The mini—*what*?" Lucas asked, but Swift quickly elbowed him in the ribs.

"Yes," the Chips' goalie said with a knowing smile. "Definitely. We'll see you at the tournament!"

CHAPTER 7

The morning was bright, with a clear blue sky and the snow seemingly edged in gold as the sun bounced off the fresh flakes that had fallen during the night. The neighbourhood in which Swift, Lucas, and Blades had found themselves once they'd left Chicken and her glorious outdoor rink looked like a postcard.

They'd left their new friend—quickly, so they didn't get yelled at again—and wandered back toward the indoor rink they'd found earlier. Luckily, the door was open this time, and there *was* an early skate (although Elizabeth Manley wasn't part of it). The Chips had snuggled up together on some chairs in a corner of the lobby, next to the vending machines, and fallen asleep.

The guy from the tuck shop woke them a few hours later, when he was opening up his little store. He sold them apples for forty-five cents each—this was 1988,

Lucas had to keep reminding himself—and offered them all free hot chocolates "to help with the kinks in their necks."

"My leg hurts," Swift said, stretching her arms high above her head. At night, she normally took off her prosthetic leg and placed it in a special spot near her bed, in the room she shared with her sister. When she kept it on for too long, the spot where it attached could sometimes swell up. Not only had she slept with her leg on last night, but she'd also slept in her hockey gear, on an uncomfortable plastic chair.

"Let's get up and walk around a bit," suggested Lucas, thinking that might make Swift's leg feel better. He checked his comm-band: "It's almost . . . 8:15 a.m."

"Already?!" yelled Swift, suddenly jumping to her feet and scooping up her backpack. "We're going to miss the tournament!"

❧ ❧ ❧

Mayhem, thought Lucas. *Absolute mayhem.*

Near the bottom of the ski jump, where Chicken had asked the Chips to meet her, a crowd of kids had gathered. Some were half-dressed in hockey gear, and all were moving and talking loudly. In the middle of the commotion was a sweaty, red-faced man with a megaphone who looked like he was about to lose it.

"LISTEN! JUST LISTEN FOR A SECOND!" the man shouted into the megaphone, but it didn't seem that anyone could hear him.

He had lists and seemed to be trying to match the names on them to the kids in front of him. His biggest problem was that the kids from a team called the Shaunavon Badgers only had nicknames on the backs of their jerseys—nicknames like the Cowboy, Rock-It . . . and *Chicken*.

One of the red-faced man's sheets blew away and he chased it down, stomping so hard on the tumbling paper that it tore in half—one part sweeping away, the other trapped under his boot.

"*LISTEN UP!*" he screamed into the megaphone. "*WE NEED ALL REMAINING PLAYERS TO GATHER TOGETHER! NOWWWWWW!!!*"

Lucas turned to Swift, his eyes wide open. "*This* is the mini-Olympics?"

"Keep it simple, stupid," she deadpanned, knowing this gathering was anything but simple. *What in the world is going on? Why is this so disorganized?*

"Chicken's over there," said Blades, pushing herself up on Lucas's shoulders a little so she could see through the crowd. There had to be at least four or five teams of players all gathered around the megaphone. Swift, Lucas, and Blades were on their way to join them when they finally got a whiff of what was *really* happening at this tournament.

"I gotta get out of here! I'm gonna—" one of the kids ahead of them mumbled before turning, tripping over a friend's stick, and then throwing up into a small bucket he'd been carrying with him.

Another kid saw him, and he, too, started to gag.

"We need that bucket back over here, *now*!" a voice called out from the crowd. It was Chicken's voice—the same one they'd heard while skating on that amazing rink surrounded by stars. Only now, she sounded urgent—like a TV doctor working in an overcrowded emergency room.

"EVERYONE WITH FOOD POISONING," the man with the megaphone was saying, "YOUR BUSES ARE LINING UP AROUND THE CORNER. A TOURNAMENT DOCTOR WILL BE THERE TO CHECK YOU OUT. AND THEN YOU'LL ALL BE GOING HOME."

In one hand, Chicken had a roll of garbage bags, and in the other, she had her own paper and pencil. As she checked on the kids who were throwing up or just looking ill, she marked their names down.

"Go to the buses if you're *actually* sick!" a young girl with thick glasses yelled, trying hard to make herself heard. "But if you're just puking because you saw another kid puke, then please *stay here*—WE NEED YOU!"

Swift was shocked as she watched the sickness move through the crowd like a wave.

Are the teams too sick to play? she wondered. *Are they cancelling the tournament?*

Once Chicken was close enough to talk, Swift grabbed her arm. "You're not calling it off, are you?!"

"No, no! But we might need to—" Chicken started. With an embarrassed smile, she held her list out so Swift could see all the names in the sick column. "Look," she continued, "a bunch of kids went out for dinner last night and got food poisoning. I didn't go—I stayed to skate on the Desmonds' rink—but our goalie and backup goalie were there. And . . . well, now they're sick."

"Both of them?" Swift asked, knowing how serious that was.

"Both of them . . . ," said Chicken. She paused for a

second and then looked Swift square in the eyes. "You guys aren't actually here for the tournament, are you? You can't have a team with just three players."

"We're . . . *not*," said Swift, careful about which words she chose. "We're . . . uh, we came here to — "

"Oh! Oh no!" moaned Lucas. Both Swift and Chicken turned to him immediately, but Chicken was the first to realize that Lucas's moans had nothing to do with hockey. The Chips' centre had one hand clutching his stomach and the other held up in front of his mouth. His face was white — no, it was turning green.

"Lucas!" Chicken called, grabbing his shoulder.

"Close your eyes — *now*!" Swift shouted.

She was afraid of heights — and she wasn't too happy that their meeting place had brought them to the ski jump again — but she'd forgotten that Lucas was afraid of something far, far worse.

Barfing.

More specifically, other people barfing.

And at this moment, they were surrounded.

"Everyone's making everyone else sick," said Blades, her mouth twisted in disgust. "You'd better not puke on me, Top Shelf."

"Well, he can't have food poisoning," said Swift.

"It's just the—*yuck!*—it's the crowd. We've got to find somewhere to sit him down."

Chicken handed Lucas a garbage bag, and Swift and Blades hooked their arms in his and led him over to a small pile of snow.

"Put your head between your knees and breathe slowly," Chicken told him. "It'll pass. Don't worry. Just concentrate on your breathing."

"You should be a doctor," said Lucas. He looked up with a smile and then quickly put his head back down.

"What I'd really like to do is to play hockey—*today*," said Chicken, waving to a tall boy and the girl with the thick glasses, both of whom were now making their way toward them. "There's no way we're letting them cancel the rest of this tournament."

"How many players have you lost?" asked Blades.

"Too many—and we've got no one to play goal," said Chicken, sounding worried. "We're lucky our semifinal was yesterday. But now how on earth can we play for the gold medal?"

"Chicken!" the girl with glasses called, glancing at Lucas on his snow mound, his head still between his knees. She held up a backpack like she was showing it off, smiled at Chicken, and then raised an eyebrow in

Lucas's direction. "Wait—is *this* their goalie?"

"Noooo. Swift plays net," Lucas replied with a hiccup, without even lifting his head.

"Okay, rad—another girl!" said Chicken's teammate, obviously a little relieved. She was now looking at Swift. "So what did you say? Are you going to join us?"

"Join you?" asked Swift, confused. She was only in novice. *These guys are already ten years old—and in atom!*

"Yeah, join our team," said the tall boy, taking off his toque to reveal a mass of curly dark hair. He was wearing his hockey jersey, but for some reason, he also had a plaid shirt tied around his waist, like some kind of fashion statement. "You know, *play* in the tournament? We need you."

"All I told them was that I'd met another goalie last night," said Chicken, raising her hands with an embarrassed shrug. "I never promised you'd play."

On the back of the new girl's jersey was the word "Ace," and on the back of the boy's, it said "Butter." But it wasn't their nicknames that had made Swift's jaw drop—it was the fact that she was standing there in front of three atom-level players, being asked to save their tournament!

"Uh, *yeah* she'll do it!" said Lucas, suddenly

pulling himself up with the help of Blades's arm.

"All right, wicked!" said Ace excitedly. She snatched her teammate's list from her hands to look at where they stood, and then quickly looked up from the page. "But, Chicken, we're down *another* forward—a good one. Squish is on your sick list!"

"I know," said Chicken sadly.

"And I just passed Farts, who was on his way to the buses," added Butter, kicking at some snow near Lucas's feet. "That's another player."

Squish? Farts? Swift let out a snort-like giggle. She couldn't help it. This team had the most ridiculous nicknames she'd ever heard.

"We need players, guys. Big time," said Chicken.

"No duh," said Ace, unzipping her backpack. She was smiling like a politician as Butter moved in closer to shield her from view. Once she was hidden, Ace pulled something from her bag and reached her arms out toward the Ice Chips' goalie.

Her mind racing, Swift wrapped her hands around the yellow-and-black jersey she was being given.

"All right, *I'm in*," she said shyly, a smile spreading across her face. "But you're going to need more help than just me. You got two more of these?"

CHAPTER 8

"That girl with the glasses asked me where our team *is from*," Blades said with a laugh, glancing over at her sister, who was on the other side of the small boiler room they'd found, tying her purple skate laces.

The three Ice Chips were in the arena where the final game of the tournament was about to be played— and they were hiding. They didn't want anyone to see that they were swapping their Ice Chips jerseys for Shaunavon Badgers ones.

For the next few hours, Swift, Blades, and Lucas would all have to act like atom-level players from Shaunavon, Saskatchewan.

And, they'd all have new nicknames.

"I hope you didn't tell her anything," said Swift, turning around to show off the words "Shut Out," written in dark, bold letters across her back.

"When we leaped, you said we had to stick together no matter what," said Blades, annoyed. "All I told her was that we were from Riverton, and that Riverton was far, far away from here."

"Hey, how did Chicken know we weren't already signed up to play on our own team?" asked Lucas.

Swift rolled her eyes. "She and Ace are the *only* two girl players in this entire tournament. This is 1988, remember? The International Ice Hockey Federation didn't hold its first Women's World Championship until . . . wow, not for two more years! In *this* time, there's no such thing as a women's hockey league. There aren't even any female hockey players kicking butt in the Olympics—not yet."

"If we were signed up, we would have stuck out," Blades said proudly, pulling on a jersey with the word "Squish" on the back.

"I guess," said Lucas. "But hey, why do *you* get Squish?"

"Do I *look like* a Farts?" Blades snapped back with a smile. She thought it was hilarious that they'd finally found the perfect jersey for Mouth Guard, and their armpit-farting friend wasn't even there to wear it.

Lucas was, though.

Just then, the door to the boiler room swung open, letting in the sounds of the other players getting ready in the dressing rooms around the corner.

It was Chicken.

"You ready?" she said, grinning. She, too, was fully dressed for the game. "Sorry you had to change in here. Ace and I sometimes have to do that, since we're the only girls playing on a boys' team and not all the parents are cool with that—mostly the ones with the other teams."

"It's okay. It's safer if no one sees us switching jerseys," said Lucas. "We get it. But I still don't see how you think we can pull this off."

"Easy-peasy," said Ace, walking up beside Chicken, with Butter shuffling close behind. He was carrying an extra hockey glove—for Lucas, to replace the one he'd left on the ski jump. "They checked our birth certificates before everyone got sick. The players whose jerseys you're wearing have already been approved—no problemo there."

"And because our coach got sick, too . . . ," added Butter, handing the glove to Lucas.

"They grabbed my dad—a guy who drives a Zamboni—as a replacement," Ace said proudly. "He knows hockey, but he doesn't get to watch our games very often—or very closely."

"Which means he doesn't know what most of our teammates look like," Butter added with a goofy grin. "Or even which new kids joined our team this year."

"Even girls?" asked Swift nervously.

"He won't question it. My dad knows girls rock," said Ace, grinning. "So do our teammates. Now let's make sure everyone else out there knows it, too!"

❉   ❉   ❉

The crowd was already stomping its feet to Queen's "We Will Rock You," waiting for the players to step onto the ice. It was made up not just of family and friends, but also of dozens of players from teams that had already been knocked out of the tournament—at least, those who hadn't gone home sick.

This was the gold medal game everyone had been waiting for. And it was the Shaunavon Badgers against a team that had come all the way from the other side of the country: the Rink Rats.

As the Zamboni made its final turn on the ice, Swift

could tell that the players from both sides were itching to watch the puck drop.

The organizers had asked the members of all the teams to shake hands before and following their matches as a show of good sportsmanship, but the Rats either hadn't been told or had chosen to ignore it.

As the Badgers flooded onto the ice and lined up for the pre-game handshake, the Rats all skated to their own end, surrounded their goalie, hammered their sticks on the ice, and shouted—along with their parents in the stands:

"RINK RATS RULE!
RINK RATS RULE!
RINK RATS RULE!
AND THE BADGERS ARE BAAAAAAAAAAD!"

Chicken was standing just in front of Swift in the non-handshake line. She turned and smiled widely through her cage.

"This is going to be fun!" she giggled.

Swift wondered how her new friend could be so calm. When she'd seen the Rats skate out in their uniforms—beige, black, and white with a cartoon rat on the front, baring its fangs—she'd known they were trouble. So had Lucas, judging by the face he

was making at Blades. The Rats' two serious-looking coaches had crossed the ice in front of them without so much as a glance at Ace's dad—the skinny bearded guy standing alone behind the Badgers' bench.

The referee called the teams to centre ice for the faceoff, and Chicken, who'd taken her position between Blades and Lucas, skated forward. She was up against a kid with neon-green skate laces—thicker than Swift's purple ones and ten times as bright. The guy was probably lanky in regular life, but on the ice, he looked big and dangerous.

He reminded Lucas of someone, but he couldn't figure out who. It probably didn't matter. There were bullies in every town, it seemed.

A moment later, the puck was dropped and the championship game was on.

CHAPTER 9

Almost immediately, the Rats' big centre tried to barge straight through Chicken. He wasn't even thinking about the falling puck. She'd seen it coming, though, and deftly poked the puck so that it slid between the kid's green-laced skates as she ducked to the right and then swung around to pick it up.

Chicken began skating down ice, her head up and swivelling to either side as she checked for her wingers. She moved the puck back and forth on her stick as gently as a new parent cradling a baby. Lucas and Swift were still fascinated by her ability to do this without looking. *Magic again.*

Chicken crossed the Rats' blue line and turned sharply, circling and drawing one defender with her—a friendly-faced kid who was quick with his blade.

While the other defender raced to cover Swift's sister, Lucas was left wide open. Chicken saw this and sent a perfect saucer pass that landed with a slap just in front of him, sliding perfectly onto the blade of his stick.

Lucas was alone. He looked up to see where he might shoot—and somehow lost the puck, the black disc slipping off his blade and dribbling helplessly into the corner.

He could feel his feet go out from under him! He fell backwards hard, first crashing into the goalpost and jarring the net loose, and then spinning into the boards behind it.

The big Rats' centre stopped hard, bringing his green-laced skates together, spraying snow and little ice chips through Lucas's cage and into his eyes.

"Oh, sorry there . . . Farts!" he said, making a fart sound with his mouth and not looking sorry at all. In fact, he was grinning. "You stepped on my stick!"

He said this loudly enough that the referee heard and seemed to agree, though Lucas knew for certain he hadn't even lifted his skates off the ice as he'd glided in on net.

The official asked Lucas if he was all right, and Lucas said he was as he rose onto his knees with Blades there to help him to his feet.

"He dumped you deliberately," she said, her face red with fury.

"You're going to have to be more evasive on the ice—keep away from him," said Chicken.

"I know," said Lucas. "I'm trying."

"Don't worry, we'll get our revenge on the scoreboard," said Butter, skating up with a smile and tapping Lucas's stick.

Next shift out, that's exactly what happened. Ace, who'd swapped with Blades in the change-up, took the puck behind the Badgers' net and bounced a pass off the boards—just as Coach Small always told the Chips to do when facing a hard forecheck. The puck slid into the skates of Chicken. She neatly clipped it over to Lucas, who was skating hard up the far side.

He wasn't going to lose *this* puck. He felt rather than saw Chicken blow past him, her wind rippling his jersey, and he lobbed the puck past the defender on his side—the nice one. Chicken roared so quickly past the defenceman that he spun and fell, leaving her alone with the puck over the Rats' blue line. She faked a slapper and the opposing goalie came out to cut down the angle, but Chicken held the puck. Then in an instant, she'd already swept around the hapless goaltender and tucked the black disc into the net.

1–0.

On the next series of plays, the Rats' centre collided hard with Swift, knocking her off her purple-laced skates and onto her butt. Again, it looked deliberate to Lucas, but the centre dropped his stick and had such a sheepish look on his face as he leaned over to help Swift up that the referee again bought that it was all just a mistake.

Swift, however, was hurt. It was her wrist—and there was no other goaltender to take her place.

"Hey," Chicken said quietly as she skated over and put her cage up to Swift's, "he's a bully. You're going to have to try to outsmart him. C'mon—brains over brawn."

Swift nodded. She knew this. If playing against Beatrice had taught her anything, it was that bullies, too, had their weaknesses.

The Rink Rats moved ahead at the beginning of the second period, and then Chicken scored once more and Lucas got a surprise goal, putting the Badgers up, 3–2.

The Rats' big centre won the next faceoff—and that's when he made his move.

He got the puck back to his defence—that nice kid, who Lucas now noticed had "Small" written across his back. *(No wonder I like him!)* Small then circled back, passing the puck back and forth with the Rats' other defenceman, waiting.

The big kid then turned, moving deep into his own end, and suddenly burst full out for centre ice!

With a nod to his teammate, Small used his stick to tip the puck up onto its side. Then, going to the backhand, he flipped the puck so high in the air that it seemed for a moment as if it were going to hit the scoreboard.

But it didn't. It flew over the heads of all the Badgers and fell behind their defence, bouncing. It was just far enough ahead of the Rink Rats' charging centre that it didn't make him offside as he came roaring in on Swift like a charging bull.

The Badgers' only goalie set herself to block the shot. But no shot came. The Rats' centre raised his stick for a slapshot, but then brought it down and used a toe tuck to move the sliding puck away from Swift. As the centre passed the net, he was able to roof a backhand in behind her.

3–3.

They were tied!

86

CHAPTER 10

Ace's dad said nothing about the play when Lucas's line came off. Chicken sat with her head between her knees as if everything were her fault. Blades said nothing. Swift looked crushed.

Lucas felt a tap on his shoulder—the coach—and expected to see an angry face, but instead Ace's dad just leaned in and whispered, almost into his own beard, "Remember that play. It worked once, so they'll try it again."

Early in the third period, the Badgers moved ahead after Chicken scored on a fabulous end-to-end rush. She'd pulled the Rats' goaltender out so far that he was sliding into the corner when she tapped the puck in.

It was 4–3 for the Badgers when the Rink Rats did indeed try that play again.

Small and the other Rats' defenceman were slipping

the puck back and forth, seemingly waiting for something, when Lucas took off. He'd seen the big centre make his turn and he knew what was coming.

But Lucas wasn't chasing the puck, and he wasn't chasing the guy with the neon laces. He was skating hard back into *his own end*. Lucas could see Swift staring at him through her mask, her eyes like the dots below question marks.

The crowd gasped as Small once again hoisted the puck high toward the scoreboard. Lucas and his teammates watched the black disc floating high through the air and saw the green-laced bully barrelling through the centre.

The puck, spinning end over end, came down and slapped on the ice just in front of the big kid's outstretched stick.

Only this time, he didn't pick it up. Instead, the Rats' centre watched helplessly as Lucas poke-checked the puck just enough to send it between his opponent's skates. The big Rat tried to turn instantly and lost an edge, going down hard and sliding down the ice toward the Chips' goalie.

Swift skated to the side, allowing him, spinning and red-faced, to crash into the back of her net.

Had this Rat been a puck, it would have been a goal. Had he knocked the net off its moorings, it would have been a whistle. But neither of these things happened. The Rats' most threatening player merely ended up tangled in Swift's net, angrier than ever.

Meanwhile, Lucas was soaring toward the Rats' blue line, the puck dancing on his stick as if he were working a yo-yo.

And his head was up! He was seeing the entire ice! He could see Ace hurrying along the far boards. He could see Chicken cutting across centre toward him.

Lucas didn't have to look down. He could *feel* the puck. He might be in a packed, brightly lit arena, but he could just as easily have been out on the Desmonds' backyard rink, playing under the Milky Way.

His puck *could* have been invisible. Seeing it no longer mattered.

Lucas and Chicken made eye contact. Neither one looked down. The puck was over to Chicken and then back to Lucas before anyone who was actually watching it could blink. Lucas leaned on his back leg as the sound "*KIIIIIIISSSSSSSS*" escaped his lips—a reminder. He moved as if going for a wrister, but instead quickly sent it back to Chicken. They'd read each other perfectly.

Chicken had roofed it into the net before the goalie even realized the puck had changed hands.

The Badgers' bench exploded, as did the packed arena. Blades and her linemates leaped over the boards, racing across the ice and falling onto the other Badgers, who were already piling on top of Chicken. Everyone was laughing and cheering.

The horn sounded: the Badgers had won the mini-Olympics by two goals!

CHAPTER 11

The big Rats' centre, still down in his opponents' end, slowly got to his feet and slammed his stick so hard over the Chips' net that it shattered like a snapped toothpick. With the broken handle still in his hands, he angrily hurled it over the glass into the stands, narrowly missing a couple of teenagers.

Stickless and fuming, the big kid circled the rink, giving two thumbs down to the crowd, but they mostly ignored him—they were too caught up in the Badgers' win. When he reached Swift and Chicken, who were grinning with their arms around each other's shoulders at centre ice, he brought his skates together sharply, sending a spray of snow through the air.

"Purple laces are *dumb*," the bully sneered at Swift, looking down at her skates. "And you play like a *girl*."

Swift and Chicken looked at each other—Swift

trying hard to stifle a laugh. Chicken had no idea what to say back.

But Blades did. "If you mean we play like girls who win," she said, skating up with a smirk on her face, "well, then—"

There was a whistle. The referee was calling for the end-of-match handshake, and this time, *all* the players were lining up—all except the Rats' sulking centre, who instead turned sharply and skated off the ice! He slammed the gate so hard behind him that the glass rattled from one end of the ice to the other.

"What a sore loser!" Lucas said, shaking his head as he moved down the line behind Chicken, slapping shoulders and grasping hands.

"He can be," said the Rats player named Small, who was coming from the other direction. The kid seemed embarrassed by the big centre's actions, but Lucas still had the feeling that they were friends.

"Why are you defending him?" Chicken asked, frowning.

"He's a good player. And he's nice to the guys on his team," Small answered.

"But he got *so mad* at me," said Swift. "Does he not like to play against girls?"

"We don't have any girls in our league," Small said apologetically. "But I'm sure he'll get used to it. Blitzy's okay once you get to know him."

The three Ice Chips froze.

Blitzy?!

As in . . . Blitz?!

That Rat had been so easy to spot with his bright laces that none of the Chips had even *looked* at the name on his jersey!

Swift sucked her breath in sharply. "No, *couldn't* be!"

❖ ❖ ❖

The big moment had arrived.

The players from both teams had been asked to form a single line on the ice, and a red carpet was being rolled out in front of them. As the crowd watched, the tournament officials stepped out onto the carpet in their shoes, followed by a photographer and a few young kids carrying fancy-looking trays piled high with gold and silver medals.

"Check them out—wow!" said Chicken, leaning her head forward so she could get a better look. "They're just like the Olympic ones!"

Once her ribbon was hung around her neck, Chicken placed the gold disc between her teeth, as if to take a bite out of it. She smiled for the photographer, giggling.

"They're not chocolate, you know," Ace laughed. "Would you do that with a real Olympic gold medal if you won?"

Chicken puffed out her cheeks, popping them in disbelief. "Sure, but do you think that could ever happen?"

"Ha, you *wish*! If these were Olympic medals, none of you *girrrrls* would get one," shouted a Rats' player from down the line—Chicken couldn't tell which one.

She hadn't seen the shouter, but Swift and Lucas had. Blitz had returned. His coach, red-faced with embarrassment, had brought him back from the dressing room.

"You know what?" Swift called. "We'll get that wish."

She hadn't bothered to wish on Chicken's stars last night; she already knew what the future held. In Swift's time, the country's hockey-playing women hadn't just made it to the Olympics—they'd brought home the gold. Over and over again. "Play like a girl," she knew, would later be said to the men's Olympic teams—not to insult them but to raise their level of play. Playing like a girl was a good thing.

Swift smiled over at Chicken, who was staring down at the gold medal around her neck, and felt a bit sad that she couldn't tell her any of this.

Not surprisingly, the silver medal Blitz had been forced to accept had already fallen to the ice with a clatter. Leaving it there like a forgotten candy wrapper, the bully had stormed off again toward the dressing room.

❖   ❖   ❖

Blades was trying to sound nice—even helpful—as she stood in the snow, shouting. Swift, however, could barely hear her sister over the roar of the crowd that was gathering—fans who were sure they were about to witness Olympic history.

"Look! I said, *LOOOOOK!* You need to keep your eyes *open* this time!" Blades called as she and Chicken pulled Swift along by her elbows, careful of the goalie's injured wrist. They were trying to find the best spot to watch the action.

To celebrate their win, Ace's dad had brought the whole team to see Eddie the Eagle, the British ski jumper, compete. And Swift's sister seemed to be the most excited of all the young hockey players.

Why? Because Swift still hadn't decided if she was going to play on the Riverton girls' team. And Blades had finally figured out how to convince her!

"This is the best *ever!*" said Chicken, shaking with excitement. "Look at Eddie up there. Does he look nervous?"

"He's waving. And now it looks like he's bouncing—or dancing a little," said Lucas, who had just appeared through the crowd behind them, followed by Ace and Butter. "This guy is awesome!"

The Chips' goalie still didn't want to open her eyes. It had been terrifying to watch this guy jump from above, but from below? If this daredevil skier fell again and broke his leg, they'd be right there to see it. Hear it. *Feel* it.

The fans were cheering—no, roaring—more than they had for any other jumper. Some people were even laughing. Eddie wasn't likely to win—most of his training had been without a coach or the right equipment—but he'd definitely caught the attention of the crowd.

Being smaller than most of the people who had gathered, the Chips and Badgers found they could duck down and wriggle through the legs and heavy winter coats to work their way to the front, where some orange mesh fencing marked off the landing area.

"You know, my cousin Doug plays in the NHL — for the Vancouver Canucks," Chicken said, almost to herself. She had her hands resting on the top of the fence and was keeping her eyes on Eddie. He was standing again, giving another excited wave to the crowd. "Doug says you have to work really hard to get there."

"And you have to *want it*," added Blades, as if she knew what she was talking about.

Swift's cheeks turned red. Slowly, she opened one eye. Then the other.

"Are you saying I don't work hard enough?" she asked her sister, her face flushed.

"No — *no*. Not at all!" Blades shook her head. What she was trying to say wasn't coming out right.

At the top of the jump, Eddie slid down his bench. He checked his bindings one at a time.

"You work hard. Everyone can see that in your game," Chicken said with a smile.

"But if you want to play hockey at a higher level, you have to be ready to fight for it — the way Eddie up there fought to be here," said Blades. "And the way

Chicken fights to play on a boys' team, even with jerks like Blitz around."

"I've grown up playing with the boys," said Chicken. "You have to have a thick skin if you're going to play hockey, and you can't always choose who's on the ice with you."

She looked over at Blades, and suddenly Swift knew exactly where they were taking this.

Beatrice. That's what this is about.

"You told her about the girls' team!" Swift said. She was a bit angry, but also a bit relieved. She'd been afraid to talk to Chicken about the decision she was facing—but at the same time, she'd really wanted to know what her new friend thought.

"If you love hockey, *play* hockey," said Chicken. "On a boys' team, on a girls' team—who cares?"

"Exactly!" added Blades, her eyes on the top of the ski jump. "You just have to play, Swift. Hockey is *your* game."

Eddie the Eagle was pulling his goggles down over his eyes. He was vibrating with energy, almost twitching, and he was rising to his feet. The crowd gasped as he suddenly pushed off with his arms behind him. He'd let go! The British skier went flying down the

snowy trail with a long *swiiiiish*, and a moment later, the jump had launched him toward the clouds.

Eddie, who'd fought for his Olympic dream no matter how many people told him to quit, was flying.

He looks a little like a Canada goose, Swift thought, not even realizing that she was watching, unafraid, her eyes wide open. *But he looks like a happy one.*

When Eddie landed, slightly off balance but on both skis, the onlookers erupted into wild cheers. The unlikely athlete was full of smiles as he skated toward them, flipped off his bindings, and raised his skis above his head with pride.

"Ed-die! Ed-die!" Ace and Butter began shouting, and the chant quickly swept through the crowd. Everyone was saying it. Everyone was feeling Eddie's moment.

No gold medal, but no broken legs either. He'd done it!

He'd competed in the Olympics!

Blades spoke loudly into Swift's ear with a lump in her throat. "If you let bratty little Beatrice *Blitz* stop you *this easily*, you'll never reach your dreams."

Swift looked at her sister and then back at Eddie the Eagle, who was now just a few feet away . . .

Just in time to see him wink in her direction.

CHAPTER 12

"DID I HEAR SOMEONE SAY 'BLITZ'?"

The voice that had just broken through the cheering was one the Ice Chips knew far too well.

There was no question: this *had* to be Henry Blitz, coach of the Riverton Stars and owner of the Blitz Sports Complex, back when he was just ten years old. *But how? And why?*

Blitz most definitely wasn't a hero to any of the Ice Chips. Probably not even to some of the Stars.

But who else could be such a jerk on the ice? Who else had *this* big an ego?

"We weren't talking about *you*," Swift said truthfully, eyeing Blitz's crooked grin and his puffed-out chest. The applause of the crowd had died down a bit as another ski jumper—one who wouldn't win and wasn't as much of a lovable underdog as Eddie—was preparing to go.

"Sure you were," said Blitz with an annoying grin. Lucas shook his head and Blades rolled her eyes.

"Aww, sweetie, were you scared for little Eddie, the ski jumper?" Blitz asked in a baby voice, looking straight at Swift. Behind him, Small was standing there in his very 1980s haircut—*Is that what they called a mullet?*—shaking his head. He had a silver medal around his neck, and another one in his hand.

"Not . . . really," Swift answered, but she'd missed a beat and Blitz could guess why.

"You're not afraid of heights, are you? Don't tell me you're . . . *chicken*?!" Blitz asked, laughing. He wasn't just playing the bully—he was acting like the kind you'd see in a movie. He was trying so hard that Lucas almost burst out laughing.

"No, *I'm* Chicken," corrected Chicken, making a motion toward Small's hand. "Are you afraid to wear your medal or something?"

"Not afraid to wear it," said Blitz. "Don't need it. I'm a gold-medal player. We all know you *girls* cheated me out of that today."

"You could at least carry it," Small complained to Blitz in a tiny voice, holding out the silver medal. "Keep it and put it in a drawer at home. You don't even have to look at it."

"Nah, it's worthless. Give it to the cheaters," Blitz nearly spat as the crowd suddenly erupted into cheers. Eddie the Eagle might have won the hearts of the crowd, but the ski jumper from Finland, Matti Nykänen, had just landed his third gold medal!

"Wait, I don't get it. How did we *cheat* you?" Swift asked.

"Well, Purple Laces, *you're* not supposed to be here," said Blitz, trying to stand his ground against a wave of exiting fans.

For a second, Swift wondered if Blitz somehow knew that she and her friends were time travellers whose home was in the future. But then she figured it out: he meant *girls* weren't supposed to be here.

"You're cheating. Hockey's for boys—and silver's for losers," Blitz hissed. He reached out as though to take the medal from Small's hands, but then he batted it to the ground instead.

"If we have to buck the system to play," said Chicken, crossing her arms, "maybe the system is wrong."

"It's not our fault you can't beat us," said Ace.

"Oh, yeah? I can't beat you?" Blitz asked loudly, stepping forward and puffing his chest out even more. "We'll see about that."

Butter quickly moved in closer to Ace, and Chicken did the same.

Lucas swallowed hard.

Is Henry Blitz going to fight us?!

CHAPTER 13

"The timing has to be just right," Chicken whispered. She was crouched behind an Olympic banner that had been hung on one of the fences. "I still think this is a bad idea, but if you have to do it, you'd better do it properly."

"This seemed like a better idea than fighting each other," said Lucas, raising an eyebrow. Blitz had given them a choice between a fight and a dare. And Lucas had chosen the dare, since he hated fighting—both on and off the ice.

The bully, of course, was delighted.

Now, instead of brawling with Blitz (*and his teammates? Would Small really have done it?*), the three Ice Chips were about to act out Swift's scariest nightmare ever.

They weren't just taking the elevator *down* from

the ski jump, as they'd done when they first landed; this time, they were making their way to the top!

Once the Chips had accepted the dare, they'd slipped off their Badgers jerseys, handed them back to Chicken, and pulled their Ice Chips ones over their heads. They'd also given Ace and Butter the three gold medals they'd won.

"For when your teammates get over their food poisoning," Lucas had said, feeling proud that they'd got to be part of the Badgers' gold-medal win.

"I'd go up with you, but the Desmonds are expecting me for dinner," said Chicken apologetically. She was carefully lifting the bottom of the fence for Lucas, trying not to look suspicious. Blades, who'd already gone under it, had just buzzed his comm-band to say the coast was clear all the way to the chairlift—their only way back to the elevator.

"I wish you *could* come," Swift said with a smile, knocking Chicken gently with her elbow as they watched Lucas scurry across the snow on his hands and knees. "But I get it. You wouldn't want to miss your last night on that awesome rink under the stars."

"Ditto. But I can't miss that rink. Tomorrow I'll be back in Saskatchewan, and you'll be home, too . . ."

Chicken said shyly. Butter and Ace had already gone back to the houses where they were staying so they could pack.

"Right, going home . . ." Swift answered, but she had no idea if that was true.

"Promise me you'll give that girls' team a chance when you get there, okay?" Chicken asked with a little smile.

"You mean play, even if it's hard?" asked Swift. She couldn't stop thinking about that team, about how Lucas's mom had called it "a great opportunity," and about how she'd been letting Beatrice Blitz ruin it.

"*Especially* if it's hard," said Chicken, her smile widening. "Remember: keep it simple, stupid."

"I will, stupid," Swift said with a giggle as her comm-band buzzed twice—the others telling her it was her turn to go.

"Pinky swear, okay?" Chicken said, holding out her little finger so Swift could wrap hers around it in a mini handshake.

"Girls' hockey will get better in a few years. I mean, it will . . . exist. I'm sure of it," Swift said awkwardly as she gave Chicken a quick hug and slipped away under the fence.

* * *

"It's going to be dark soon," Lucas said, pointing toward the sky, which had turned a yellowish orange. The wind had become colder, too. The three Ice Chips were hiding behind some bales of hay, watching the metal lift sweep up the hill in front of them, one chair after another clinking by.

"I'm going to miss her," said Swift. She knew she'd never forget Chicken—the girl with the invisible puck.

"Me, too," said Lucas.

"Guys," said Blades, peeking around the hay. "The man running the chairlift has gone to get his picture taken with Eddie. And he's left the lift running . . ."

"Great, so when do we—" Swift started to ask, but she wasn't sure she wanted to hear the answer.

"The chairs go through the bottom of the lift every seven seconds or so," said Lucas, checking his comm-band. "I've been timing them."

"Do we go now?" Blades demanded, poking her head over her bale of hay for another look. "He'll come back."

"No," said Lucas nervously. "Okay—WE GO NOW!"

The chair dipped slightly as it pressed into the backs of the three Ice Chips' legs and they sat down. It was sweeping them off their feet.

"Blitz is still down there, watching us," Blades said. She turned around as their chair rose into the air. "What a jerk-a-doodle!" Another one of Edge's made-up words. (If he ever did play-by-plays, he'd obviously be amazing.)

"Look at him," Lucas laughed, leaning over the bar of the chair and looking back down the hill toward the thinning crowd. "Blitz thinks he's winning—thinks we're scared."

"I *am* scared," Swift said, her voice shaking.

The moment Blitz had suggested the dare, Lucas jumped on it. It made sense: each time they'd leaped, they had to go back the way they came in order to find their way home. Lucas was now sure of it. Somewhere up there, high above the crowd, a wormhole was waiting for them.

As the chair rose higher and higher, Blades couldn't get over the view. The sunset was turning pink and purple, and lights were popping on all over the Olympic Park, making it look like a snowy fairy land—a place where magic happens.

"I'm sorry we didn't get to meet your hero," Swift said to her sister, shifting her weight to the right. With her bag beside her and her wrist aching, she was finding it hard to get comfortable.

"Nica," said Blades, trying to avoid eye contact, "*you* are my hero. I don't always like to admit it, but it's true."

"I'm *what*?" Swift asked, shocked, as Lucas let out a little giggle.

"Everyone said you should play sledge hockey because of your leg when we were little," said Blades. "That was cool, but you wanted to play standing hockey instead—and you did it. You trained and you worked and you got good. I mean, you got *really, really* good at it."

"You're probably the best player on our team," Lucas whispered, blushing.

"You have talent, but you also have heart, like Eddie," Blades continued. "You're one of the strongest people I know."

"And like Chicken said, you can't let Beatrice stop you," Lucas added, reaching into his backpack. "I found something on the ground that should remind you of that."

"Silver?" asked Swift, laughing when she saw it. "Isn't that for *losers*?"

"It's to remind you to keep trying. Not to let anything stop you—not even a Blitz," said Lucas, placing the medal in Swift's hand.

"I'll treasure it," she said, giggling. She wrapped her fingers around the ribbon—at the very same moment their chair started to rock . . .

With a rusty, creepy, grinding sound, the chair swung violently to the right, then to the left, spilling the silver disc out of Swift's hands and over the edge of the chairlift.

"*Nooo!*" Blades and Lucas both yelled.

But the Ice Chips' goalie, acting on instinct, had already gone after it.

❋ ❋ ❋

"HELP ME!" Swift yelled with panic in her eyes. She'd caught the medal in one hand and was desperately dangling from the chairlift bar with the other.

"Hold on!" Blades gasped as the chair swung in the other direction, creaking like it was about to fall.

"Blades, she's slipping!" Lucas called.

Swift was holding on with only the tips of her fingers . . . when Blades suddenly caught her by the arm.

Blades could see the fear in her sister's eyes: she couldn't grip back—her wrist was too hurt.

"Give me your other hand!" Blades yelled. Lucas reached for Swift, too, but the chair suddenly swung back again—creaking, threatening—and tossed him toward her sister instead. Now Lucas was holding Blades and Blades was holding Swift, whose entire body was dangling from the chairlift, far above the snow and lights.

"Can we fall into the snow from here?" Lucas asked, freaking out. "Do you think she could drop?"

But Blades had another idea.

"What if we just rock it *more*—rock her back up? Swing the chair so she can get her leg up onto it, then you can grab her around the middle?"

Lucas thought it was risky, but he didn't have another plan.

"Okay—on three," he said, securing a hand on one of the bars and the other on Blades's arm.

"One," said Blades, rocking the chair as hard as she could to the left without letting go of her sister's hand.

"Two," said Lucas, making it swing the other way — so far that Swift's leg could almost reach it.

"Three!" Blades, Swift, and Lucas all shouted at the same time as the chair swung back again.

That's when they heard the top of the chair — the part where the metal wheel meets the metal wire — unhooking, screeching, moaning . . .

Suddenly, it was as though the floor had been pulled out from under them.

And they were falling!

CHAPTER 14
Riverton

Blitz's silver medal was the first thing to hit the ice. It appeared, as though out of nowhere, skidding across the red line of the Riverton rink, and hit the boards with a clack. Next came Swift and her teammates, followed by their bags and sticks. Lucas and Swift were aware they'd just come across the centre line on Scratch's perfect sheet of ice—they knew how it worked by now—but at the same time, they could swear they'd just fallen out of the sky.

It had all happened in slow motion.

The chair on the ski lift in Calgary had tipped one final dramatic time; it had creaked and stuttered as it tilted. The supporting bar had become unfastened. They'd dropped about a foot with a quick jolt. And then, one by one, the Chips had lost their grip . . . they'd let go.

Falling—Swift first, then the others—they'd watched in horror as they sped through the cold, twilight-filled air toward the hard-packed snow beneath them.

The fairy lights had grown brighter and brighter, and were soon bleeding into each other—almost glowing.

And then the feeling of falling had given way to floating.

Instead of being dropped, they felt more as though they'd been launched.

Like Eddie.

Like an eagle, pushing off and taking flight.

And when the lights had unblurred themselves and separated, they'd become the reflection of the rink lights in Scratch's perfect flood.

Miraculously, nothing was broken, nothing hurt—except for Swift's throbbing wrist.

The Chips were still breathing heavily as they dusted themselves off and changed out of their equipment. A moment later, they were already headed for the WhatsIt Shop.

Crunch, Mouth Guard, and Bond would definitely want to hear about this leap. But they'd also want to hear the amazing news: Swift was finally saying yes to the girls' tournament!

❊   ❊   ❊

To Lucas's eyes, the fix-it club looked more like a take-it-apart-and-make-a-big-mess club. All he could see through the front window of his parents' store was junk—odds and ends piled high on the cafe tables, surrounded by smiling faces. There were almost a dozen kids using little hammers, glue guns, and screwdrivers, all under the supervision of Lucas's mom and Quiet Dave the Ice Man.

Not far from where Dave was sitting—keeping an eye on him—was Crunch. The Chips' science guy was painting two blue lines and a red one on that old cookie sheet Lucas's mom had helped him find.

"Okay, I'll play on the girls' team—*I'll do it!*" Swift blurted out as she approached them. Then, to Dave, she added, "You can tell your daughter I'm in!"

Over by the glue guns, Lucas's mom broke into a gigantic smile. "Do you want *me* to call the mayor?" she said gently, trying to contain her excitement. When Swift nodded, Lucas's mom just opened up her mouth and yelled: "Abigail!"

Stepping out from one of the aisles, her arms piled high with tubing, was the mayor, showing off the biggest smile the Chips had ever seen. She'd already heard Swift's final decision!

"We're old friends," Mrs. Finnigan said with a playful shrug.

"I'm so glad to hear you say that, Swift," Mayor Ward said, with what looked like tears welling up in her eyes. Swift knew this tournament meant a lot to the mayor, but she was still surprised to see how much. "Most of the other towns have had girls' teams for years, but we've never had enough players to form one."

"Until now," said Swift, suddenly feeling the weight of her decision, the importance of it.

"Until now," the mayor agreed, beaming.

* * *

"Do you think Dave *knows*?" was Lucas's first question after the WhatsIt Shop's cafe had been cleaned up and the last of the neighbourhood kids had spilled out into the chilly evening air. "Hey, do you think he could *tell* we'd just leaped again?"

Lucas was glad his mom had let him walk home through the snow with his friends. They had so much to talk about!

After the Chips' first leap, Dave had told Lucas that time travel was dangerous and he should never do it again. Lucas had promised that he wouldn't, and now he'd broken that promise—twice.

"Well, it wasn't a pinky promise, was it?" said Swift, laughing, remembering the funny handshake that Chicken had taught her.

"Maybe the magic of the rink has made Dave *forget* that you leaped?" offered Mouth Guard, squinting his eyes like he was looking into a crystal ball.

"I told you, it's not magic!" complained Crunch, who was dragging a garbage bag behind him on a sled. Mouth Guard had just told them all he thought there was a wizard in the wormhole who waved a magic wand to send the time-travelling Chips flying through the air.

"Just wait until you see the rink model I'm building," said Crunch, ignoring his teammate and glancing back at the bag of fix-it inventions he was towing.

"Wait until *you* see the new trick we just learned," said Swift, throwing her arm around her sister's shoulders.

"Yeah," said Lucas, punching Edge lightly in the shoulder. "*We're* the wizards now. And the moment we hit the rink, we'll show you how to make your puck invisible!"

* * *

Swift and Blades were in their beds with the lights off when Lucas and Edge buzzed.

It was the middle of the night, but the boys were calling from the outdoor rink behind their school. Lucas said they'd stuffed their beds with pillows so they could sneak out—"for a skate under the stars."

Of course, both Swift and Blades knew what that really meant: training, Chicken-style.

"If you're already on the ice, you're not giving us much of a warning," Blades said loudly into Swift's comm-band.

"We didn't want to bother you," Lucas said sheepishly. He was thinking about the girls and their tournament, and about how they'd better be in good shape for their team's first practice the next afternoon—especially because the Ice Chips already had a practice scheduled for that morning.

But it turned out that he needed their help.

Lucas could still *do* Chicken's trick of shuffling

the puck back and forth, as quiet as if he were stick-handling a sponge, but he had completely forgotten how to explain it.

"My wrist still hurts," said Swift. "I need to rest it up for tomorrow—I can't come out."

"Can you just—" Lucas started, but he wasn't quite sure what he was asking. "I'm trying to get Edge out of his slump."

"Are the stars out right now?" Swift asked, slipping her prosthetic on and walking over to the window to part her curtains.

"Yeah," said Lucas.

"Then keep your eyes on the night sky," she said confidently. "You can make a wish if you need to."

Swift was nervous about tomorrow afternoon's practice, but she was also excited. *It's too bad Chicken can't play with us now*, she thought—almost wished this time—looking up toward the Milky Way. *Is it possible that Chicken—wherever she is—is still looking up at the same stars we are? Where could she be?*

CHAPTER 15

On his way into the Riverton Community Arena for the morning Ice Chips' practice, Lucas had followed his usual tradition. He'd run his hand along the lip of the skate sharpener's shop, straightened the picture frame on the wall beside it, kissed two of his fingers and pressed them against the glass of the trophy case.

Same as always. Only this time, it wasn't.

Just as he was placing his fingers to the glass, his eye caught something in the top right of the photo of the kids hoisting the championship trophy high above their heads.

"It *can't be*," he said, blinking and shaking his head. Swift and Edge were now staring, too, but they couldn't figure out what had him so excited.

Lucas was almost shaking as he pointed to the banners hanging on the wall in the background of the photo: three second-place ones that said "Ice Chips," four for the Stars (the Stars had since taken their banners with them to their fancy new rink), and one that said—

Impossible!

"What is it?" asked Edge. "You can't believe the Ice Chips won their division a few times but won the championship only once? We've talked about this a hundred times, Top Shelf."

"No, it's—" Lucas started, barely believing what he'd spotted.

Swift swallowed hard. She could see it now, too.

"How could it be—?!" she called out, slapping a hand over her mouth in disbelief. They could barely make out the words on the first banner—the oldest one—but neither Swift nor Lucas doubted what it said.

Peering down over the heads of the kids in the photograph, baring its fangs and smiling, was a big, mean-looking . . . *rat*.

* * *

"Did a team called the Rink Rats used to play here, in our arena?" Lucas asked Coach Small from the bench.

The Chips' centre had slipped out of practice to get Swift some ice for her wrist and was now helping her hold it on her arm while the other Chips continued their practice. Looking around the rink, he couldn't shake the image of the Rats' banner that had once hung from the rafters.

"Yeah, sure," Coach Small answered, like it was nothing. He banged on the boards and gave the Chips another drill.

While Coach Small was directing the practice, Quiet Dave was poking his head in and out of the little room suspended above the rink, where the music for the figure skaters was played. He was trying to get everything set up so Edge could call the shots for the girls' first team practice that afternoon.

"But *when* did the Rats play here?" Lucas asked his coach, just as Dave blasted the rink with a few seconds of rock music and then turned the volume down.

Coach Small ignored them both; he was busy pointing to different areas of the rink, explaining a play. To Lucas's surprise, it was Mayor Ward, who'd been watching their practice from behind the bench, who replied.

"The Rats played here a long, long time ago—in the 1980s, I guess," she said, almost laughing as she brushed her bangs out of her eyes. "They were the first team to have this rink as their home ice, you know. They were good, even if they *were* a little show-offy at times."

Show-offy, Swift thought, rolling her eyes. In the change room, she'd been told who the girls' coach would be—Coach Blitz—and that was already making her regret joining the team. Her wrist was feeling a lot better from the icing, but the idea of playing for Blitz was making her head hurt.

"Blitz the bully," Swift mouthed at Lucas, nudging him with her knee.

"What happened to the team?" Lucas asked, ignoring his friend.

"Well, after they won their division—and got that banner—a whole bunch of kids decided to sign up for hockey," she said as she started flipping through pictures on her phone. "That was the year my dad and I moved here."

"Everyone wanted to sign up, so they *cancelled* the team?" asked Lucas, confused.

Dave was now waving from the little room with the microphone. "We've got music—sort of!" he yelled to his daughter as another quick blast of a rock song rained down over the players on the ice.

"No, they *all* wanted to sign up, so they broke the Riverton Rink Rats into two new teams—the Ice Chips and the Stars. Oh, here it is!"

The mayor handed her phone to Lucas and Swift, who each held on to one end.

What she had was a copy of the picture in the trophy case, and this time, Lucas and Swift could zoom in.

"There's Coach Blitz," said Mayor Ward, pointing at the two Ice Chips holding the trophy over their heads. "And that's Coach Small beside him. Ugh, I'll need my glasses if I'm going to tell you everyone."

They really were *friends,* Lucas marvelled, staring at their arms over each other's shoulders, the gold medals around their necks.

"Your mom joined the Chips the next year, Lucas. Otherwise, she'd have been in this photo, too," the mayor said, smiling. She found her glasses in her pocket and finally slipped them on. "We played together for a few years—she was good."

Lucas knew his mom had once been an Ice Chip, but he'd never really *thought* about what that meant. *Was it hard for her back then? Did Mom dream of winning the championship, too?*

"Oh, and there's me," the mayor said, turning to

the two Ice Chips with a big smile on her face. The kids looked down to see the face of a ten-year-old girl wearing thick dark-rimmed glasses, just like the ones the mayor had on.

Swift gave Lucas another nudge. Lucas nodded slowly, but his eyebrows were raised as high as they could go.

The little girl with the medal around her neck, posing beside the trophy . . . they knew her, too!

"But you're—" Swift started, just as Dave hit them with another blast.

"Edge, get over here!" the Iceman yelled triumphantly across the ice—he'd fixed the sound system! As the town's new play-by-play announcer laid down his stick and quickly made his way over, Lucas and Swift could see that Quiet Dave was beaming proudly at the mayor—his daughter, and the woman who, before moving to Riverton as a ten-year-old, had been a killer winger for the Shaunavon Badgers.

❖　❖　❖

"Can you believe all of that?" Swift whispered to Lucas, once she'd put down the ice and was back doing drills.

"Blitz even had those green laces in that photo! How could I have missed that?" said Lucas, almost talking to himself. "When we were back in Calgary, I had the feeling I'd seen them somewhere before!"

Suddenly, the doors of the arena swung open and in marched Henry Blitz—it was almost as though Swift and Lucas had summoned him.

"Small!" he yelled as he made his way across the rink with Beatrice skipping behind him. "I need an assistant for this *girls'* team. You wanna come help me out?"

Coach Small looked up, but he didn't say anything. *They aren't friends anymore,* Lucas reminded himself, though he had no idea what could have broken them apart. Well, some idea.

"Hold on—the Ravens need an *assistant* coach?" Blades yelled back, stopping fast in front of her sister. "*I* know who would make a good one!"

Swift looked at her sister, confused.

"Stick together, remember?" said Blades with a wink.

"Who?" asked Coach Blitz, smirking.

"You!" she told him, grinning defiantly.

Swift expected Beatrice to stick her tongue out at Blades, but instead she seemed to be trying to hide a smile. *Is that possible?*

"Well, that doesn't—" Coach Blitz didn't know what to say. "Then who would . . . ?"

Of course, Lucas and Swift knew exactly *who*. They were staring right at her.

The mayor of Riverton.

Or as they'd known her back at the Calgary Olympics: *Chicken's best friend, Ace.*

CHAPTER 16

Swift, Blades, and Bond were sitting on top of their packed hockey bags in the snow, watching the sun rise over the Riverton Community Arena. They'd been told to be ready early. The plan was to have all the girls from the Chips, the Stars, and Riverton's house teams — together, the Riverton Ravens — on their chartered bus by 8 a.m., and on their way to the Hopedale tournament.

But the girls weren't the only Ice Chips about to board the Ravens' bus; some of the boys were going, too. Lucas had been "hired" by Mayor Ward to be an assistant for the Ice Chips players, in case she had questions about their strengths and weaknesses, or they needed special help with their equipment. Crunch was going as the team's amateur statistician, and Edge, now giddy that he was out of his slump, was finally getting his chance to do the play-by-play for a game. Mayor Ward had promised there would be a microphone waiting for him at the Hopedale rink.

As they sat waiting for the bus, Swift couldn't help thinking about the unbelievable week they'd had. They'd leaped into the 1988 Calgary Olympics, seen Liz Manley and Eddie the Eagle, and met an amazing girl named Chicken, who'd taught them an incredible trick. And . . . well, they'd also learned a lot more about Henry Blitz, who, as a full-of-himself ten-year-old, had hated the idea of girls playing *his* sport.

And now, here they were in the present, part of a Riverton girls' team that was off to the Hopedale tournament!

I'd like to know what Blitz thought when the first woman played in the NHL, Swift wondered with a chuckle. Manon Rhéaume, a goalie and one of her idols, had done that in an exhibition game for the Tampa Bay Lightning in 1992—just four years after Blitz played that game against the Badgers. *If only I could have seen that sore loser's face then!* Or if she'd been able to see Chicken's . . .

As the bus pulled up in front of the Riverton arena, Swift checked her backpack to make sure the precious object she'd stashed in it was still there. Then she grabbed her hockey bag, as did the other girls, and tossed it into the bottom of the bus.

"Ready to win today, girls?" Blitz asked, as he hung his head over the railing at the top of the steep bus stairs. Beatrice was tucked into the corner of the seat opposite, sitting by herself and staring out the window.

Swift had no idea what was up with her new teammate, but she did know one thing: they had a tournament to play, and they would be playing it together.

"We girls are *always* ready to win," Swift said, giving the team's assistant coach the same crooked smile he'd given her back in Calgary. She was tempted to ask Blitz what he'd thought when the three hockey players had accepted his dare and had fearlessly taken the chairlift up the mountain . . . and then never come back down. But she didn't. He had no idea the girl in front of him was the same one he'd played against in 1988, the one he'd accused of cheating for playing on a boys' team.

Instead, Swift nodded to Lucas and Bond and slid her backpack in beside Beatrice, the grumpy-looking blonde-haired girl who, for so long, had been her arch-enemy.

❧   ❧   ❧

They were almost an hour into the trip when Beatrice finally spoke. "This is just for the tournament," she said quietly to Swift, offering her a piece of the chocolate bar she was eating. "We're not really friends. We're still enemies. We still play for competing teams."

"Sure," said Swift, taking the chocolate.

During the Ravens' only practice, Swift had made a big effort to be nice to Beatrice, for the sake of the team. She knew she couldn't let her fights with the Stars' forward hold her back—she'd learned that in Calgary. And she knew that if Beatrice did well, the Ravens would, too. So Swift had taught her new teammate and Jessie Bonino, one of the house league forwards, a few new tricks: how to "keep it simple, stupid," and how to make their pucks invisible.

"Oh, hey, Bea?" Blitz said, looking across the bus aisle and using his usual bossy tone. "We'll get Jared to show you that play we've been working on when we get to the Hopedale rink, okay? He's got some great ideas. If you listen to him, I'm sure we'll bring back the gold!"

Swift couldn't believe she'd never noticed this

before. Beatrice was the league's top scorer, but to her father, she was still just a girl playing on a boys' team. *This must be one of the reasons that Beatrice wanted a girls' team so badly—so she could stop being compared to her brother,* Swift thought, shaking her head. *No wonder she's always in such a bad mood on the ice!*

"You've got some ideas? That's nice," said the mayor, jumping in. She'd been walking toward the front so she could talk to her husband, who was driving the bus. "Well, we've got a few beauty ideas of our own, don't we, Bea? Swift? I'm sure our girls will be great."

Swift and Beatrice had no idea what those ideas might be, but they nodded anyway.

CHAPTER 17

There were four rinks in the Hopedale complex, and all of them would be used for the single-day tournament. First there would be a few regular games, then a semifinal, and then a final to determine the winners of the cup.

Beatrice seemed more on edge than she'd ever been. Jessie Bonino, who'd been playing house league for only a year, was nervous, too. The two girls had their helmets pressed up to the glass to watch the Zamboni flood the ice before the Ravens' first game.

"Don't worry," said Swift, stepping up beside her new teammates. "We can do this."

"We'd better," said Beatrice, nodding with a hopeful smile.

Lucas and Edge had stopped at the tuck shop before heading in to take their seats. Lucas was behind

the Ravens' bench, chewing on some licorice and ready to help if needed, and Edge was munching on a bag of chips over at the "media" table, where he'd be calling the plays for the game.

Mouth Guard, Lars, and Crunch—the Chips' math nut was now armed with a notepad and that silly cookie sheet he'd been calling his "model"—were in the stands. And not far from Lucas was Jared Blitz. He, too, was behind the Ravens' bench, working as the equipment guy for the Stars' girls. Lucas could hardly believe that he was now hanging around with the very player who had butt-ended him, but like Swift, he hadn't had much of a choice.

Soon, with a loud "AND THEY'RE OFF!" from Edge, the puck was dropped.

To the shock of most of the girls on the team, the Ravens won their first match easily. Blades played on a line with Beatrice and Jessie Bonino, and Bond played defence with Shayna Atlookan, another Stars player. Swift, of course, was in net. She was always in net.

In their second match, against a team from Montreal, the Ravens were again surprised, this time winning in a shootout. Beatrice, scoring the winning goal in a nail-biter, had even used the invisible puck trick to fake out the goalie!

"*Aaaaaand* it's Beatrice Blitz with the *Bliiiiiiiiiiiiiiiitz-krieg Bop!*" is what Edge yelled into the microphone as the other boys cheered, danced, and sang the Ramones song that went with it—one of their favourite rink tunes. Not even Mouth Guard, who loved to point out the obvious, had to mention that it was a goal.

The games were shorter than usual and the tournament moved along faster than Swift had expected. Still, she found she needed to rotate and stretch her wrist during pauses. She knew she should ice it, but there was just no time.

Next came a team from Ottawa. They were the Novice Sens, and they wore black-and-red uniforms that looked like kid-sized Ottawa Senators jerseys. They had four coaches, all in suits.

The Sens were flashy and well organized. Even their entrance onto the ice seemed to have been rehearsed a million times.

This was the game that would decide if the Ravens made it to the semifinals.

By the end of the first period, Henry Blitz was already angrier than the Chips had ever seen him. And when Blades was called for tripping one of the Ottawa players, he turned so red he looked on the verge of blowing hot lava out of his ears. Luckily, the mayor—the team's *real* coach—said he had to either calm down or go home. There was no place for that here.

When their assistant coach took a long breath and then tried to give them instructions again, all Swift could picture was the red-faced ten-year-old who had smashed his stick over her crossbar at the Olympics long, long ago.

"We have to give the girls some room to make choices for themselves," Mayor Ward warned him. "Step back a bit and let them figure it out."

Ace played with Blitz for all those years, thought Lucas, overhearing. *She obviously knows how to handle him . . . and knows how to get him to back off.*

Of course, it was Beatrice—even after she'd scored another winning goal, this time against the Sens—who still had to figure that out.

CHAPTER 18

By late afternoon, the largest of the four rinks in the Hopedale Sportsplex was packed with fans, most of them coming from Riverton and High Falls—the two towns to make this semifinal.

Lucas, Jared, and Edge were all in their places off the ice when the High Falls Hornets skated out to loud cheers from the crowd. Next were the Riverton Ravens.

Swift was first on the ice, and Edge knew he had to make the most of it.

"AND HERE'S THE RAVENS' TOP NET-O-NATOR, THEIR QUICK-GLOVED DETONA-TOR . . . NICA 'SWIFT' BERTRAND!"

"He's really funny," Jared said, laughing like he couldn't help it.

"Yeah, well, he's my best friend," said Lucas with a shrug, but obviously feeling proud. He wondered if

Jared might be feeling the same way about his sister. "Beatrice is killing it on the ice," he offered, smiling.

"She is," said Jared, grinning back. "I hope this helps my dad see that she's the best player out there."

"Even if *he* doesn't know it," said Lucas, watching the crowd, "everyone else does."

The Ravens fans were on their feet, wildly cheering as the players got into their positions.

Swift skated fast to her net. She tapped both goalposts with her stick and went into a deep crouch, backing all the way into her net like an ocean crab burying itself in the sand. Then, with a simple push of her skates, she slid out past the crease and turned sharply to her left.

Before the puck drop, the Hornets all gathered around their goalie, went quiet, and then broke their huddle with everyone shouting "Win!" together.

The Ravens didn't have a handshake or a call yet, so instead, Beatrice Blitz reached out and smacked her stick into Swift's pads. The two girls looked at each other. It had only been a week since Beatrice had deliberately "run" Swift with the intention of injuring her. Now they were teammates. Now they were working together.

"*KIIIIIIISSSSS*," Beatrice said with an awkward smile.

Swift, surprising herself, smiled back easily. "*KIIIIIIISSSSS!*"

* * *

By the end of the first period, the Hornets were ahead 2–1. Beatrice Blitz had scored the Ravens' only goal, with an assist by a surprised Jessie Bonino. The High Falls Hornets were well coached. Swift could tell they were putting out their strongest skaters each time Beatrice stepped onto the ice—and there was nothing she could do about it.

She'd also noticed something else: her teammates were using the same breakout play every time—and the Hornets were blocking it. Bond, on defence, kept trying to stickhandle her way out to the blue line before passing, but the High Falls kids had been instructed to go hard on the forecheck, sending skaters in every time Bond had the puck behind her own net. That meant she had to fight her way through a jungle of stick checks and blocks before reaching the blue line, and it just wasn't working.

The score remained the same all through the second period, with the Riverton team spending much of the time bottled up in their own end. Mayor Ward knew that the spectacular play of Swift and Beatrice was the only thing keeping the Ravens in the game.

After the horn blew to call an end to the period, the officials decided it was time for a scrape—one that would delay the game for a few minutes. The mayor, relieved and knowing she had to change their strategy, leaned forward over the Ravens' bench.

Swift was there with her mask raised so that she could spray some water into her mouth. She was so wet from sweat that it looked like she was coming out of a pool, not off the ice.

"We can't score," Swift said, meeting her coach's eye. She was exhausted. Disappointed.

"I think we can," said Mayor Ward, glancing down at Swift's purple-laced skates. "I'm not sure why, but I'm thinking about a move I saw years ago, during a game I played in Calgary. I think it could work."

Swift looked up at her, puzzled.

"You girls are getting forechecked to death," said Mayor Ward. "Bond can't skate through the whole team to get the puck out of your end. You've got to try this trick." She lowered her voice to explain the play—it was Blitz's move from 1988, but with a slight change.

"Huh?" Swift asked, her eyes blinking in confusion once the mayor was done. Of course she knew this shot, but . . .

"Bond will hoist the puck high over everyone's heads. Beatrice will be expecting it. And then we'll send it to Jessie for the shot—and your sister Blades for the distraction. It will look like an easy play at first, but at the very last second, we'll fake out their goalie."

"But that's not keeping it simple," said Swift. She'd seen the move—Blitz's move—work. But adding in nervous Jessie? Could the house league player handle it? Could her sister?

"We're taking a simple move and making it better," said the mayor, with almost a mischievous grin. "You guys have been playing simple so far, which is what they'll expect. It's time to buck the system a little."

Swift nodded. She shot some water full into her face, shook off some of the drops, and then pulled down her mask sharply.

The scrape was over and the referee was blowing his whistle for the start of the third period.

They were going back on the ice.

* * *

Before they formed up for the faceoff, Swift quickly called Bond and Beatrice over to her crease. Lucas could see that the Ravens' goalie was very animated. She had her mask down so it was impossible to read her lips, but he could tell what she was saying from her body language: pretending to lift a puck backhanded, using her glove hand to demonstrate a high arc in the air. At the end, she tapped Beatrice's jersey to let her know the next step was up to her, and leaned in to whisper something.

Just before the faceoff, Beatrice nodded back toward Jessie. Mayor Ward was talking to Blades at the boards.

The Ravens won the faceoff but soon lost the puck to the Hornets, who seemed by far the stronger and more confident team. The Hornets regrouped in their own end and began a rush.

They came across the Ravens' blue line on a three-on-two with only Bond and Shayna between them and Swift. The Hornets' forwards formed a triangle so the puck could be dropped back and the final forward could get a good shot away—perhaps even one that Swift wouldn't see coming.

That forward took her shot, but Swift tracked it all the way, holding up her blocker to send the puck flying harmlessly into the corner. Blades picked it up and moved along the side before rimming it back along the boards to Bond, who had moved behind Swift's net.

The Hornets sent in two forecheckers, anticipating that Bond would once again try to lug the puck out to the blue line.

But the Ravens had another idea. As the two forward checkers came in, Bond went to her backhand and sent the puck as high over their heads as possible.

Beatrice was waiting for exactly that moment. The puck slapped down on the ice near centre, and she was away on a clear breakaway.

Beatrice came in hard on their opponents' goaltender. She faked once, twice, then stretched the goalie out as the Hornet tried to cut off the short side.

But Beatrice didn't shoot. Instead, she held the puck and swept fast around the Hornets' net, coming out the other side with the goalie trapped against the far post.

Jessie was coming in fast as Beatrice shot the puck over to her, invisible-style. Meanwhile, Blades, the distraction, suddenly skated across the blue line in a full

figure-skating arabesque, her arms and legs stretched out behind her!

Jessie Bonino, her nervousness gone, was able to quickly and quietly tap the puck in, without a single sound.

The crowd stood, in shock. *Did that really happen? Could this brand-new team really pull off such an awesome, bizarre move?*

The fans didn't know what to say, but Edge did.

Even before the buzzer had sounded, the words were already out of his mouth.

"BONINO! BONINO! BONINO! BO-NIIIII-NOOOOO!"

CHAPTER 19

"My wrist is killing me," Swift told Lucas as she skated up to the bench and slowly removed her glove. The score was 2–2 and the referee had just called for sudden-death overtime. Players on both teams could feel the tension, and each one of them knew she'd have to step up her game.

"You're playing differently," said Lucas, leaning over the boards toward his friend. "Your wrist must be throwing you off."

"There's not much more to go," Blades said from the bench, giving her sister a quick pat on the shoulder.

"This will be tough," said Swift, rubbing her hand around that wrist, trying to loosen it up by adding some heat. "But I can do this."

Beatrice skated up, trying not to look over at her father. "Ugh, we're never going to make the *final*!"

she said, seeming stressed. "If we don't win this, we're done. That's it!"

"We're not done yet," said Swift, carefully replacing her glove as the referee's whistle blew again.

Beatrice was looking down at the ice as she skated back into position.

"That was a good move," Henry Blitz called over in his daughter's direction, while she was still close enough to hear it. He hadn't moved from where he was standing. He'd taken Mayor Ward's advice and was trying to give the girls some room—especially now that he'd seen what they could do. The "rafter puck" was a move he'd used before, but never, *ever* so brilliantly.

"Thanks for that," said Beatrice, surprised. *Really? No advice? No telling me to be more like Jared?*

"You're doing amazing out there," said Henry Blitz, banging on the boards. He was no longer looking at her like she was just his daughter—but like she was also a real hockey player. The fact that she was a girl didn't seem to matter anymore. "The Ravens are great, Bea—no matter what happens from here on in."

Back on the ice, Swift thought the Hornets seemed more focused than the Ravens, but she wondered if the pain in her wrist was just confusing her.

Beatrice had her game face on, but the Hornets won the faceoff easily. Almost immediately, Swift was blocking their shots again—but just barely.

"You're favouring your sore wrist," said Bond, as she sent the puck out from behind their net. She wasn't the only Raven who'd noticed that Swift's game had changed—and the Hornets had seen it, too.

"I think I'm scared to hurt it more," said Swift. "I can't stop thinking about it."

Even from the other side of the rink, Beatrice could tell what Swift was saying. And this time, *she* was the one with the idea. She was too far away to tell her new teammate, but she was close enough to Edge at his "media" table to have him pass on her message.

It took only a second for Edge to get it. And then, as the Hornets snagged the puck again and their forwards moved into formation, the Ravens' play-by-play guy pulled the microphone closer to his mouth.

"This is a tense moment. Nothing's decided yet," he said more quietly than usual. "If this were an outdoor game, both of these teams might be WISHING ON THE STARS!"

Swift looked across the ice at Edge, then at Beatrice, who was nodding.

The Ravens' goalie understood immediately. She was heading for a slump, just like Edge's. She was thinking too hard, watching the puck too closely. And her hurt wrist was making her lose her instincts.

Am I really going to do this? she wondered.

Slowly, Swift closed her eyes.

She stopped thinking and started feeling.

Soon, she could hear the puck being scraped up off the ice; she could even hear it moving through the air.

And somehow, as if by magic, Swift now knew where that puck was headed, each and every shot.

CHAPTER 20

It was dark on the country highway, with black-looking pines lining the road like the border of some dark enchanted forest. The only lights were from the few cars that passed the Ravens' bus and then disappeared into the night. A light snow had also started. The mayor's husband, a tall, friendly guy with a mass of curly dark hair and a plaid shirt hung over the back of his seat, kept having to turn the windshield wipers on. They were now causing a dull scraping sound as they cleared the wet snow that had stuck or melted onto the windshield—a sound that was making Swift feel sleepy. Of course, that made sense. This entire day had already felt like a dream.

The Ravens' goalie could barely believe that she'd kept her eyes closed through their sudden-death overtime against the Hornets, but she had. She'd acted as though she had a blindfold on. It was almost as if Chicken were there, instructing her under the stars.

This was Beatrice's idea—and the hint that Edge had given her over the loudspeaker.

Without her sight, Swift seemed to have *felt* the puck with some other part of her brain. She'd *sensed* it. And then she'd blocked that puck—over and over again!

At least, she'd blocked it until the Hornets had got a penalty and Henry Blitz had convinced the mayor to pull the Ravens' goalie to give their team a two-man advantage.

That's when the Hornets had scored. And *that's* when the Ravens had lost both their semifinal and the tournament.

In the end, the score was Hornets 3, Ravens 2— but the players from Riverton had definitely made an impression. They were a real team, with real skills and a goalie who could stop a puck just by listening for it. With the help of Beatrice Blitz, Swift had taken Chicken's puck trick and made it her own. *Goalie magic.*

Sleepily, Swift looked up at the television mounted at the front of the bus—the show on was about past Winter Olympics. In a flash, there was Eddie the Eagle, flying through the air, then a men's speed-skating final, and then Canada's Olympic women's hockey team, winning gold for the very first time. The players were jumping on each other and cheering. They had the biggest smiles Swift had ever seen. Riverton's only female goalie's heart always fluttered whenever she saw one of these inspiring stories. She loved watching athletes' dreams come true—sometimes in a single moment or a single game.

Did we really *see an Olympics in Calgary?* Swift wondered as the bus continued along the road home.

Up on the television, the Olympic rings faded away to show the hosts of the show around a table.

"How did you feel at that moment—the winning moment? What did that mean to you? And to the women on Team Canada?" one of the hosts asked their special guest. The camera turned to that guest—a blonde female hockey player with bright eyes and a friendly smile.

Swift did an immediate double take.

On the lower part of the screen, letters identified her: "Hayley Wickenheiser, four-time Olympic gold medallist."

Hayley, the hosts went on to say, had retired from her amazing career in hockey to become an emergency room doctor.

Only, the player was no longer just Hayley Wicken-heiser to Swift—one of her idols, one of her all-time greatest heroes.

The Riverton goalie had finally put the pieces together, and now her cheeks were flushed with both embarrassment and pride.

Hayley Wickenheiser was . . . *Chicken.*

The bus was still rolling through the night when the mayor started working her way down the aisle, congratulating each of the Ravens' players. She didn't care that they hadn't made it to the finals, or that they hadn't won anything they could bring home.

They had no medals, but they'd *played.*

They had existed.

For one amazing little tournament, Riverton had had its girls' team. The first. And they hadn't com-pletely tanked. For the girls who'd come out to play, *that* had meant everything.

"You played wonderfully, I hope you know that," said Mayor Ward as she got to where Swift and Beatrice were sitting—the same seat they'd taken on the way to the tournament.

"But we didn't get a medal," Beatrice said, nearly under her breath. She had crossed her arms and was

looking out the window again. Swift couldn't tell if she was sad or just mad at herself.

"We'll talk about that next practice," said the mayor, leaning over her husband's shoulder to get a look at the snow and then looking back again. "You'll be there, right, Swift? Beatrice? What we did out there was big—no matter how the game turned out."

"You mean that's not the end of it?" asked Beatrice, surprised.

"Not even close," said Mayor Ward with a gigantic smile. She let Beatrice turn quietly back toward the window but gave Swift a high-five, and then continued to give them down the line, all the way to the back of the bus.

"*Beatrice?* I've got something for you," Swift offered shyly, tapping her seatmate's leg. "But you, uh, have to keep it a secret, okay?"

Slowly, she unzipped her backpack and pulled out the silver medal she'd been hiding inside—Henry Blitz's medal, the one he hadn't wanted back at the mini-Olympics in Calgary.

"It's silver," Beatrice mumbled.

"Yeah, well not everyone can have gold," said Swift, remembering the big Rat's attitude—throwing his broken stick into the crowd—when he found out his team had finished second.

"Sorry, I mean it's great. Silver is great," said Beatrice, correcting herself. "We didn't win anything at this tournament, so of course silver is great."

"You can keep it until next year, as a placeholder," offered Swift with a smile. "Keep it until we can win our own. Or five, like Hayley Wickenheiser—she got four gold and a silver, too."

"You think we ever will get our own?" asked Beatrice.

"We'll start earlier next year, and we'll hold more practices," said Swift. "We'll still be Chips and Stars, but we'll be Ravens, too. We'll just have to work harder than usual."

Beatrice suddenly looked excited. "You think the Ravens could have a chance at the final?" she asked.

"More than a chance," Swift answered confidently. "Bea, we're just getting started!"

ACKNOWLEDGEMENTS

Thank you to our editor, Suzanne Sutherland, whose name might not be on the cover, but whose careful work and guidance are visible on every page of this book. Thanks to Maeve O'Regan in publicity for her encouragement, and to Editorial Director Jennifer Lambert for her support. Thank you to the rest of the amazing team at HarperCollins, who allowed us to feel where this book should go and helped us get there: Janice Weaver, our eagle-eyed copyeditor; Stephanie Conklin, our patient and efficient production editor; and Lloyd Davis, our careful proofreader. Thank you also to Bruce Westwood and Meg Wheeler at Westwood Creative Artists, for their guidance and friendship.

Thanks to the many friends and new acquaintances who lent us their stories so we could shape the characters on the Ice Chips team, especially Gabe

Ferron-Bouius, an impressive goalie from Ottawa who taught us how he's adapted his butterfly for his prosthetic leg, and Harnarayan Singh, for coming up with his Bonino call just in time for Nick Bonino's Stanley Cup playoff goal.

And a huge thanks to Hayley Wickenheiser, for putting up with our questions, giving us some insight into her years as a young peewee player, and being awesome and inspiring in so many ways.

—Roy MacGregor and Kerry MacGregor

Many thanks to Roy MacGregor and Kerry MacGregor, for creating another adventurous story to illustrate; to Suzanne Sutherland, whose amazing talents brought everything together once again; to Kelly Sonnack, for being my amazing agent; and to the 1988 Olympic ski jumps, for sticking around long enough to draw from—I will miss you.

—Kim Smith

Roy MacGregor, who was the media inductee into the Hockey Hall of Fame in 2012, has been described by the *Washington Post* as "the closest thing there is to a poet laureate of Canadian hockey." He is the author of the internationally successful Screech Owls hockey mystery series for young readers, which has sold more than two million copies and is also published in French, Chinese, Swedish, Finnish, and Czech. It is the most successful hockey series in history—and is second only to *Anne of Green Gables* as a Canadian book series for young readers—and, for two seasons, was a live-action hit on YTV. MacGregor has twice won the ACTRA Award for best television screenwriting.

Kerry MacGregor is co-author of the latest work in the Screech Owls series. She has worked in news and current affairs at the CBC, and as a journalist with the *Toronto Star*, the *Ottawa Citizen*, and many other publications. Her columns on parenting, written with a unique, modern perspective on the issues and interests of today's parents, have appeared in such publications as *Parenting Times* magazine.

Kim Smith is an illustrator from Calgary. She is the *New York Times*–bestselling illustrator of over thirty picture books, including *Boxitects*, the Builder Brother series, and the Pop-Classics picture book adaptations of popular films, including *Back to the Future*, *Home Alone*, and *E.T. the Extra-Terrestrial*. Growing up, Kim's favourite hockey player was Lanny McDonald. She still admires his iconic moustache to this day.

MORE ICE CHIPS MAGIC!

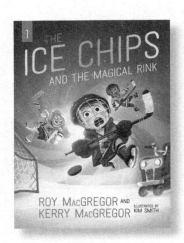

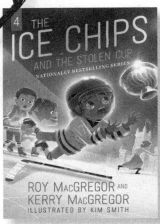